Sahil Will Come & Other Stories

Afsar (Mohammad) is a bilingual poet, writer, literary critic and scholar working on Hindu-Muslim interactions in India, especially Andhra and Telangana, Muslim writing and Telugu culture. Recognised as an important, trend-setting contemporary poet, he has published five volumes of poetry in Telugu, a collection of Telugu short stories, and critical essays. Afsar has won several awards for his writings in Telugu and English. His published works in English include *The Festival of Pirs: Popular Islam and Shared Devotion in South India* (2013); *Evening with a Sufi* (2022), a selection of his poems translated by Afsar with Shamala Gallagher; and *Remaking History: 1948 Police Action and the Muslims of Hyderabad* (2023). Afsar teaches South Asian Studies at the University of Pennsylvania, Philadelphia.

Alladi Uma and **M. Sridhar**, former professors of English at the University of Hyderabad, have been working collaboratively in translation between Telugu and English for three decades now. Their work has been widely published; recent translations include *Sorajjem* by Akkineni Kutumbarao (2016); *How are You Veg? Dalit Stories from Telugu* by Joopaka Subhadra (2021); *Asprishya Ganga and Other Stories* by Kolakaluri Enoch (2021); and *Telugu: The Best Stories of Our Times* edited by Volga (2022). Their sensitive translations, with a focus on caste and gender, have won numerous awards, including the Jyeshtha Literary Award (1993), Rentala Memorial Award (2006), and Malathi Pramada Sahithi Puraskaram (2018). They are currently involved with the Alladi Memorial Trust that works with the education, health, and legal needs of the underprivileged.

Sahil Will Come & Other Stories

Afsar

Translated from the original Telugu by

Alladi Uma *and* **M. Sridhar**

Orient BlackSwan

SAHIL WILL COME & OTHER STORIES

ORIENT BLACKSWAN PRIVATE LIMITED

Registered Office
3-6-752 Himayatnagar, Hyderabad 500 029 (Telangana), India
e-mail: centraloffice@orientblackswan.com

Other Offices
Bengaluru, Chennai, Guwahati, Hyderabad, Kolkata,
Mumbai, New Delhi, Noida, Patna

First published by Orient Blackswan Private Limited 2025

ISBN 978-93-5442-691-9

042438

Typeset in
Adobe Jenson Pro 11.5/13.5
by Le Studio Graphique, Gurgaon 122 007

Printed in India at
Avantika Printers Private Limited, New Delhi 110 020

Published by
Orient Blackswan Private Limited
3-6-752, Himayatnagar, Hyderabad 500 029
e-mail: info@orientblackswan.com

Contents

Acknowledgements

We have dabbled in translation for a little over thirty years now. In this long journey, we have worked with many Telugu writers, mainstream ones, writers from the Left, Dalit writers, writers from the BC communities, writers representing minority voices, and with women and men representing each one of these groups. Working with each one of them has been unique and a learning experience for us.

Working with Afsar, especially with this volume, has been singularly different. For someone who has been writing and publishing extensively in English now, we wonder if he should have allowed us to translate his work. We thank him for reposing trust in us. He has been extremely patient from the time we started translating these stories in 2020 till now when we can see the end product on the horizon. He has got back each time a clarification was needed, in record time, be it from us or the editor. It has truly been a collaborative endeavour. Thanks a lot, Afsar.

We guess it is not easy to work with "experienced" translators. As an editor, Moyna Mazumdar has put up with our idiosyncrasies, while giving into some of them, even as she had her own ways of persuading us without explicitly saying so. Thank you, Moyna.

Nilanjana Majumdar! You have known us for years, and you knew exactly how to deal with us. We cannot thank you enough. We thank Orient BlackSwan for the pleasure of working with it once again.

Working on projects like these tires the patience of everyone at home. We thank each one of them for putting up with us.

Alladi Uma and **M. Sridhar**
Hyderabad, 22 November 2024

Journeying with Afsar

Afsar is no stranger to us, nor is his work. We had translated his poem 'Again, Yet Again' for an *Indian Literature* volume of Telugu Writing in translation in 1995. His was a powerful voice in poetry that one could not gloss over. A voice that was strident yet nuanced. Content was crucial but not at the cost of poetic style. And we continued to translate some of his poems.

Now, more than twenty-five years later, this short story volume. A few years ago Afsar invited us for the book launch of *Sahil Vastadu* (Sahil Will Come). We were wonderstruck by the readings from the volume, and the critical analysis of the book by Telugu scholars. It impelled us to read it. The stories raised questions that made us sit up and think. There were no easy resolutions. There was a message or more in each story but they were not didactic. The themes ranged from fanaticism to casteism to regionalism to feminism to lesbianism to diasporic experience, to name a few. The writing technique intrigued us. The voice could only be of a person like Afsar: the introspective voice of one who was going through varied experiences. The incidents in the stories seemed to be attendant to the introspections of the narrator and the narratives read like interior monologues. Afsar's experiences as a Muslim, moving from a village to a town to a city and finally, to the US, as a journalist, as a writer, as an academic, as an erudite well-read intellectual, as one politically engaged, as one fluent in Telugu, Urdu and English, and finally as a sensitive individual.

So when Afsar approached us a couple of years ago to translate the volume, we did not think twice before saying yes. Initially, he wanted us to omit his very first story, 'Adivi' (The Forest), from the collection because he felt it did not fit in with the tone and tenor of the rest. But we felt that it gave us an insight into his varied preoccupations and concerns, that it was very much a part of his journey through different phases of his career as a writer, and we were able to convince him to allow us to include it. We are happy. And so will readers be, we believe, once they read his introduction!

Though the stories are seemingly simple, we had to grapple with their many-layered linguistic complexities. Afsar writes as a Muslim who uses Urdu, and of a particular kind, while speaking in Telugu. And for his Telugu readers he gives the meanings of Urdu words, phrases and sentences in Telugu in the text itself. How could we render such intricate yet everyday plurilingual negotiations in simple, conversational English? We decided to retain the Urdu in the text and to translate both the Telugu and the Urdu into English. To many readers this may appear to hamper free flow or readability. But wasn't this the case in the Telugu text too? We did not find this to be a problem. One of us knew Urdu and did not bother to read the translation, while the other was happy that the author had provided the translation. We thought that if this apparent disjunction did not bother us in Telugu, it should not bother readers in English either—let them too engage with and understand the essential bilinguality and complexity of the Telugu-Muslim!

The stories also posed problems in understanding their religious and cultural milieus. We have tried hard to understand and get these across in our English translation. Here too, Afsar had himself provided explanations of some culture-specific terms for his non-Muslim readers in the Telugu original. We have retained them in translation, and added a few more that we felt were necessary for a wider audience, as notes. To this end we are grateful to Afsar who was patient in answering all our queries. We wanted to retain the flavour of the Telugu original with its Urdu flavour. If the text does not sound proper 'English', so be it! No apologies given.

In 'Chhoti Duniya' (A Small World), a story based in the US, Afsar has used English phrases and sentences; we have retained these, using italics. The Urdu that Afsar uses in his stories, and which appears in our translation, is peculiar to the language spoken by Muslims in the interior Telangana region. Afsar, being a poet, intersperses his prose with frequent quotes from other poets in Urdu and English in Telugu translation. We have translated the Urdu poetry directly from Telugu, while we have gone to the original sources for the English verse.

Let us together struggle to understand and journey through the intricacies of this seemingly simple rendering of life! We hope you enjoy them as much as we did in bringing them to you.

Alladi Uma and **M. Sridhar**
Hyderabad, 23 March 2022

Before Sahil Arrived

I was in class 8 when I first experienced the satisfaction as well as the dissatisfaction of writing a story. I had just moved to a town from a village. I was in a state of utter confusion (linguistic and cultural): How do I grapple with Telugu, Urdu and English? Unable to adjust socially, unable to share my feelings, desperate and almost in tears, I turned to the Telugu alphabet. One day, instead of crying in frustration, I scribbled something down, and called it 'Story'. My friends encouraged me and I started to ink every scrap of paper I could find. I remember their compliment: "Yours is pure Telugu without a single Urdu word." With their encouragement, writing stories became my new routine. But I wrote without any idea or expectation of publishing them.

All I knew is that I wanted to write well. So I started reading everything I could lay my hands on—from Gurajada to Arnad in Telugu, from Charles and Mary Lamb's *Tales from Shakespeare*, to Somerset Maugham, to Saadat Hasan Manto in Hindi translation, and Ismat Chughtai in Urdu. Based on my readings, I wrote short stories. But I am unable to find them now.

During my Intermediate days, I met a boy called Ranga who sold waist-threads. My story 'Adivi' (The Forest), published in 1983, is based on him. My friend sent this story to *Andhra Jyothy* for a Deepavali writing competition. My joy knew no bounds when I knew it was judged by eminent writers like Kalipatnam Ramarao, Madhurantakam Rajaram, Peddibhotla Subbaramaiah and 'Smile' (Mohammad Ismail of Rajahmundry), and I won a prize! I wrote many stories after that but selected only a few of them for this volume.

From the 1990s onwards there have been many changes in me and in my views on the genre of the short story. Though I had moved from the village to the city, the village continues to be a significant part of me. I have lived in three big towns, a metropolitan city and America.

The demolition of Babri Masjid in 1992 was the birthplace of several new questions. The harmonious and peaceful co-existence of Muslims and Hindus had been broken. Urdu, never heard before in the streets, now began to sound loud and clear. The line of demarcation between Hindus and Muslims was now clearly visible. When caste-related violence in Karamchedu, Andhra Pradesh, became a harsh political reality, I turned towards Dalit identity. There is definitely a connection with this and my writings 'Ooravatali Dukham' (The Sorrow on the Outskirts of the Village), 'Yanam Vemana Emane' (What Did Yanam Vemana Say), and 'Dhedee' (2002), a story in this collection.

I do not know what my perceptions would have been if 6 December 1992 had not taken place; not that our history before Babri had not made me reflect on what being a Muslim in India meant and what being labelled as 'Turaka' signified. But after 1992, the term 'Turaka' also compelled me to confront and to engage with the antagonism and hostility associated with it.

There was a new question in my mind as to why and how the seeds of religious hatred took firm roots post-1992. It took time to ponder and digest the question. That took the shape of 'Gorima' in 2002.

My family has traditionally been Left-oriented. So I too have been influenced by the Left movement and its ideals. I have always maintained a balanced perspective towards Islam. Some of my Muslim friends would urge me by saying, "Come into the Khila where only our people live," and look out for houses there. I wanted to document some such instances after 1992, and did so quite noticeably in my poetry. Though my friends who had admired the sharpness, the intensity and the varied nature of my work did not quite welcome this change, I couldn't ignore this haunting question and experience. I started becoming more outspoken about the feelings that arose in me.

It is not surprising that my attention turned towards Muslim politics after 2000. When I was working in the Rayalaseema region of Andhra Pradesh, my association with Muslim cultural life became more intense. I took the example of cultural practices around Peerla Panduga, and wrote many articles based on my research. Those formed the basis of my book *The Festival of Pirs: Popular Islam and Shared Devotion in South India* (2013).

That was also the turning point for me, both as a researcher and as a short-story writer. I wanted to understand Sufism not only as a religious practice or a spiritual mode but as a social phenomenon, from an ordinary person's perspective, from the very beginning to the present. That Sufi illumination began with 'Dhedee' (2002), and it brought others in its wake. I realised how deep and profound a friendship the Sufis had brought about between Muslims and Dalits. This organic, syncretic, religious, cultural and political fabric was threatened when religious fanatics destroyed the tomb of the loved and venerated Deccani Sufi poet Vali in 2002. My writings since then have been a response to this, of which 'Chamkipoola Gurram' (The Chamki-Flowered Horse, 2015) is but one instance.

Some dates and the bloodshed that ensued are significant for me.

1947: Partition of the country, and the Police Action in Hyderabad
1992: Demolition of Babri Masjid
2001: Destruction of the Twin Towers in New York by Al-Qaeda, and the ensuing Muslim hunt
2002: Godhra massacre and its aftermath
2015: Lynching of Muslims that began with the killing of Aqlaq

If I could not communicate to my readers the daily predicament, turmoil and anguish of Indian Muslims, I would fail as a poet, a short-story writer, a researcher and a teacher, but more importantly as a human being.

I do not tag on Mohammad after my name, but it is nevertheless a brute fact and a haunting everyday reality for me. It is not difficult for me to say if I experienced this reality more acutely in Khammam or in Hyderabad or in the US—*not talking* about it at all is what is difficult. And I can emphatically say that I would not have experienced this anguish had I lived only in Khammam and in Hyderabad, and not moved to the US.

I have been stamped with the suspicious 'SSS' at every American airport I have passed through and subjected to hours of 'special' interrogation. Perhaps it is those hours of interrogation, significant markers of state authority and power, which forced me to acknowledge and become aware of my identity in ways that I had not done before.

This pain is obvious in the volume of poems *Oori Chivara* (At the Edge of the Village, 2009). But if one observes the trajectory of my work carefully, I think it is only after coming to America that my voice as a story writer has emerged cogently. I cannot imagine writing stories like 'Chhoti Duniya' (A Small World) and 'Sahil Vastadu' (Sahil Will Come) without my day-to-day life in America. Like the local rural rootedness experienced in 'Gorima', the trauma of the urban diasporic experience in 'Chhoti Duniya' too is localised, and it is as powerful—both are part of the anxieties that ordinary Muslims in Khammam and Hyderabad live through every day.

My journey has been parallel to and a co-journey with those of women's movements, Dalit and Muslim movements, all of which form a broad community of solidarity. Though I am involved with several identity movements, I am grateful that both my readers and my critics have recognised that I also have my own individual trajectory.

As a storyteller, beginning with 'Adivi' (The Forest) and up to 'Vachche Poye Vanallo...' (In the Intermittent Rains...), I begin every story with a question and try to find as many answers as possible. I belong to the 1980s' generation which felt that there could be no single answer to a question. I have been involved with the doubtful 1990s that followed the questioning 1980s. This journey too is a part of my stories where many questions collide and many answers meet. There may be some which end abruptly without any resolution.

I do not believe that one can imagine or conceive of ideas or even begin to think outside of one's own time. But even as we talk of the present, I also believe that, to a certain extent, every work treads and anticipates the future. I believe that there are ways by which a story truly *becomes* a story: that is a writer's technique and craft. I also believe that there exists a delicate, wonderful and magical bond between the writer who weaves the story and the reader who reads and interprets the life in the stories. Who is this person? Why did she do this? What is the freedom that he seeks? Such questions that arise in the mind of the reader are natural, and also necessary.

In the history of my family there is a firm and strong foundation for this thing called freedom. Both my mother's and my father's families had given up everything they had for the Telangana struggle and poured themselves into it. Every turn taken by the Communist Party runs parallel with the history of my family. If my mother's family was totally involved in the political field, my father's side was equally immersed in the cultural arena, as a part of Praja Natya Mandali (People's Theatre) and Abhyudaya Rachayitala Udyamam (Progressive Writers' Movement). Father always emphasised the importance of the freedom of speech and expression, irrespective of one's ideological commitment.

I have imbibed and internalised this vitality of the freedom of speech and thought from my family—so too the consciousness that the personal is political, and vice versa. You will hear this even in the Muslim voices in these stories. Seen from this perspective, it is not surprising that 'Gorima' is the first story in this collection. Once terms like 'Urban Naxal' entered our daily idiom and changed our ways of thinking, I thought of 'Sahil Vastadu' as a sign of that change. You will hear a voice of protest in each of these stories. I am confident that as long as there is love and empathy for others and for life, there will be the desire to capture the spirit of human freedom in a person's voice, regardless of their identity and social location. Each time this confidence, this faith has been derided and threatened, I have turned it into a story. This volume is a collection of many such moments.

Afsar
Philadelphia,
7 December 2018

1. Gorima

That in another hour I would be back in my village awakened all kinds of emotions in me!

As I tried to slide my gaze through the window of the slowly moving passenger train, the scorching sun did not allow me to look straight above. In the distance the dirisena tree full of red flowers looked like a red flag flying amidst a green river. If the eyes were lowered a little, there beyond the gravel stones were clusters of yellow tangedu flowers. I shook off all the glittering artificiality of city life that had settled on me and melted into that scene for a while.

Crossing those tiny platforms and moving past the trees, fields and streams even faster, the train was rushing me back into my childhood.

To those evenings that I had walked on these very platforms, holding my father's little finger. In a way, ours were middle-class migrant lives. We did not stay beyond three years in any village. Even so, why I am calling this village *my* village is because we had spent a little longer here. That short span might not be long compared to the thirty-six years of my life, but it is that "short span" that I loved very much.

I had stepped into this village with the *Qaida*, the Urdu primer I had read only at home. At first they had not allowed me to be admitted into the first class, and admitted me in the street school.

The teacher would call me "Arey you…Alif-Be!"[1] That stuck and became my name. When everyone called me by that name, "Alif-Be…what bey?" I would run to my mother in tears and I would raise a hue and cry, "I don't want this alif, be! Teach me a, aa!" I did not know then that my mother did not know these a, aas. Then father would take a slate and make me write a, aa. But amma wanted me to learn Urdu. She would make it a point to make me read the *Qaida*.

Till I was five, I did not know what my language was. When everyone was reading the first class text book, I would feel ashamed. I did not even know the fifty-six letters of the Telugu alphabet well.

My daily routine would begin with the fazar namaz early every morning. Getting up at dawn without anyone waking me up had become a habit with me. After doing vazoo, ablutions and cleansing for namaz, and wearing the topi, I would get ready to do the namaz along with my mother. I ought to mention that I loved doing the namaz. I did not know that it was a divine duty or some such thing. I loved amma very much and I would do all that she did with a lot of enthusiasm. I would sweep the house along with amma. I would clean the kitchen along with amma. I would wash the clothes along with amma. I would press the washed clothes, fold them and arrange them in the wooden almirah.

As amma did not have the job of going to school I liked all her chores, and I would get completely involved in those chores. Until the teacher sent someone every day to call me, I would pretend to forget all about school.

"Yera, Alif-Be? Do you think you are some nawab? Should attendants come to fetch you every day?" Saying this, he would whack me with a tamarind twig.

On one such occasion, when the tamarind twig was busy at work on my back, I heard a voice say, "Pantulu! What's all this… without even thinking that he is only a child?"

---

[1]**alif, be, te…:** first three letters of the Urdu alphabet.

When I turned around to see who it was, I felt as if a goddess had descended. She was looking razor sharp at the teacher and talking.

Without flinching the teacher said, "This fellow, and a child?" and he gave me another resounding whack with the twig. That was it. She charged at him like lightning, snatched the twig from the teacher's hand and broke it in two. When she broke it like that, the teacher was stunned. All the children made a huge racket. A new twig would not be handy very soon. The teacher would have to call Bhadramgadu, and he would have to go climb the tree. That meant they were all relieved of the whacks till then! Looking at the goddess who had rescued me from this teacher, I ran to her and hid myself in the folds of her white saree.

That evening she came home and abused my father and mother in a way that they would never forget. "Moti jaisa bachcha le jake wo shaitan ke pale mein dalne hath kaise aye? How could you possibly hand this pearl-like child into the custody of that demon?" In response to this harsh, angry question, my mother said, smiling, "In chilachintar. Isko ghar mein rakh liya toh ghar girako mandva dalta. Tumareko naimalom, Gorima. You don't know, Gorima. He is one big monkey. If we keep him at home he will bring the house down."

It was then that I came to know that her name was Gorima.

Though I was a bit angry and hurt at what my mother said, it disappeared with Gorima's words and I stood there playing with the kongu[2] of her white saree. Gorima appeared to me like a powerful force that could rescue me from any difficulty, like a great friend who appreciated my words, my song and play. I would always remember, now and forever, the hands of the woman who shaped my life and me.

Gorima said, "Arey bachche, tu roz mere paas aa. Mai Urdu, Arabi padatim. Child, you come to me every day. I will teach you Urdu and Arabic." Saying this, she left.

---

[2]**kongu:** also paita or pallu, part of the saree that is draped over the shoulder.

Gorima relieved me of that wretched street school. In her words I could hear the song of freedom that would let me fly and soar in the sky.

That was it. With the arrival of Gorima, my whole life changed. But I did not have the imagination or the maturity then to understand that the stream that was Gorima, who always had a smile that was like white jasmine, was dashing against rocks and flowing over boulders.

We had come to some platform. Everyone was getting off the train. I was still tangled in the web of my thoughts when I looked out and realised—this was my village and that I had to get off. I hurriedly picked up my bag and got down.

As I was about to get off the platform someone came and stood in front of me and asked, "Saar, kahan jate? Where to, saar?" Rickshaws in my village too, I thought.

"I don't want a rickshaw."

"Not a rickshaw, saar, a vehicle. You'll have to walk a long distance to the village," the man said.

"No need," I said and, as if I was preoccupied, started walking ahead.

Looking around, my eyes anxiously searched for the familiar as I wondered if I would be able to find any traces of my past. The station had not changed much. There wasn't much of a crowd. I was carefully looking at the few people there. Not a single familiar face. Then, was there anyone who was keenly looking at me? No, no one. Thinking that the village would have forgotten me a long time ago, I walked up to the station's exit. There too I paused to look in front and behind me. Silence. There wasn't even the sound of the train leaving. A couple of steps more and I would be outside the station.

As soon as I stepped out, there were three or four people begging. Wondering if any one of them would recognise me, I looked at them closely. They looked like four crazy people. One old woman had covered herself completely and pulled herself tight into a bundle. Perhaps she was ashamed of begging. Even when they begged, women of my community had to have a burkha. Of the other three, two were lame and one was blind. Humming some tune and adding his own at the end, one of them said, "Babu, please give something." I mechanically threw a rupee in front of the old woman in the burkha, and walked on.

I had just taken a couple of steps when I heard a scuffle behind me. The other three had pounced on the old woman, were beating her up and snatching away the rupee. Pulling her veil even closer as she struggled to save her rupee, the old woman was losing out. I was irritated. I turned back, yelled at the three of them, threw half a rupee at each of them and quickly walked on.

To reach the village from the station one had to walk some distance. I loved this distance. In my childhood I used to walk this distance with my father. How good it was to listen to nanna talk or to ask him questions when he did not talk just to make him talk! Usman would also come along sometimes. He could not tolerate the silence that lay between the station and our village. Trees on both sides of the road, the dusty wind that blew, absolutely no one around, a solitary house to be seen somewhere in the distance...unable to tolerate all these, Usman would start singing. It is not possible for me to describe how well he sang! And all the while he sang, I would keep looking at his throat and at the tiny beard that kept shaking. I had never asked Usman what the meaning of the song was, nor had he told me.

"Who taught you this song?" I had asked him once.

"Gorima."

Till then I had not known the musician in Gorima. Later I came to know how soulfully she sang during Muharram! And that the entire village knew about her singing!

One evening in the month of Muharram, amma was going about in a frenzied manner at home. She finished cooking quickly.

"You too eat quickly." Saying this, she made my father and me sit down hurriedly for dinner.

"Why all this rush?" asked father.

"Today Gorima is going to sing the mournful maatam[3] songs that Shia Muslims sing during Muharram."

Finishing our dinner quickly we went to the maatam. Till then I only knew of the commotion in the peerla chavidi, the house of peers. After attending the maatam, I came to know that women also observed Muharram with great zeal and frenzy. As Gorima was standing in the centre, swaying and singing, the women were moving around her in a circle, singing and dancing in frenzy! That was the first time I had heard them sing full-throated. How ecstatic she looked! Every time she sang the pallavi[4] refrain, I would jump in joy. As soon as she spotted me jumping, Gorima broke through the circle of women and came out even as she continued to sing, took me along with her and made me stand right next to her. That was it—Gorima sang, and I danced along with the other women! I was so happy to see those who would not even open their mouths in their houses, those who would not move their feet freely, singing full-throated and swaying their hands and feet freely and dancing as if they were used to it.

But my happiness did not last long.

Muharram came the next year too. But Gorima did not sing.

One evening, around the time when in just another two or three days they would install the peerlu in the chavidi, Gorima came to my mother in an agitated state. Her hair was dishevelled, her jasmine-like white saree had faded, and her eyes which would always be calm and shining were spewing red embers. Gorima was speaking in a very animated and angry tone. I could not comprehend

[3]**maatam:** funeral lamentation; for Shias it designates mourning rituals, including the singing of elegies, dirges and chest-beating, performed specifically during Muharram to honour Husain and the other martyrs of Karbala.

[4]**pallavi:** in Carnatic music the first of three parts of a composition; the main theme or refrain of a song which may be repeated.

anything from her talk. All I could grasp was that she was in great difficulty. Gorima spoke to mother for a long time, then went away. After she left I asked mother what had happened.

"You won't understand." Mother would not tell me anything no matter how much I asked.

It was only when father came home for dinner that she started telling him everything on her own. But even then I did not understand a thing. All I understood was that it was something to do with Gorima's house.

That night I could not sleep for a long time. I got up early in the morning and went to Gorima's house.

There was a lot of noise and commotion there. There were people everywhere. Shrieks and shouts. People were coming in hordes carrying plates full of flowers and coconuts. More and more kept coming. Pushing my way through all those people, I stepped into Gorima's house.

Just as much as I loved Gorima, I also loved that house. It was a large storeyed house. At the end of the house was a huge neem tree. On that tree, green and red flags. As soon as I stepped into the house, the welcome of flowering plants and their fragrance entwined me. More than them, it was Anwarbhai, who always looked like a washed pearl in his white lalchi and pyjama. But the ever smiling Anwarbhai who I saw every day was not there that day. In a house of three or four rooms, the last room was Anwarbhai's. Without thinking, I walked up to it.

Anwarbhai was lying on the floor and looking up at the roof, deep in thought.

I called out very softly, "Bhai...?"

Gesturing with his head to say, "Come," he was again lost in thought.

I went near him and sat down.

"Bhai...," I said again.

I did not know what to say. The situation there was completely strange to me. I had never heard such a silence in that house before. In fact at this time, Arabic lessons ought to have been going on. Anwarbhai ought to have been on the top floor, sitting outside reading something or watering the flowerpots. A morning without all this activity frightened me. Outside, all that din and commotion...and inside the house, such silence! As Anwarbhai did not say anything, I came out into the verandah again. Gorima had just come there, it seems. She was sitting and counting the tasbi or prayer beads. As I went and sat in front of her, she said, "Kab aaye, ba? When did you come, ra?"

Without answering her, I asked, "Kya hua, Gorima? What happened, Gorima?"

When I asked her like that, she broke down. She pulled me onto her lap and, weeping, said, "Mera ghar shaitan ke paale hua, ba. My house has gone into the hands of the devil, ra."

"Bahar kya ho raha...? What is happening outside...?" I asked.

"Shaitana kafira jame. Kyonki amma aayi katte... Some devils and non-believers have gathered. Because some woman is possessed, it seems..." As she was saying this she kept weeping, but I could not understand anything. This was not a situation I could understand even if it were explained to me. The commotion outside seemed to be receding gradually. The shrieks and shouts had lessened somewhat. Gorima waited for a while and then she went back to her namaz. I came out.

A large stone leaned on the outer wall of Gorima's house. They had smeared bright red bottu and kumkum on it. They had tied festoons around it. I had seen such a sight near the lake once. And now, here.

That stone looked horrific to me. Unable to look at it for very long, I angrily threw a pebble at it to show my extreme displeasure, and came away. From then on, that stone shape has always haunted me. I had to ask mother. If she did not know, I had to ask father.

Mother and father were sitting in the front verandah. Father was correcting exam papers. Mother was picking tiny stones from rice.

"Gorima is worried," mother was saying.

"What can she, a woman, do? Our people do not come to the aid of others," father was saying.

"Has the goddess really sprung up there?" mother asked.

"What's all this about goddesses springing up? Doesn't the house look good? Some fellow must have eyed it! He must have planted a stone there and vanished, that's it. Aren't we crazy about stones? If it has bottu and kumkum on it, then naturally someone would get possessed!"

Listening to their conversation, I was about to sit down in a corner when father saw me and said, "Where did you go, babu?" and drew me close. I went and sat next to him.

"The village president listens to you, right? Why don't you put in a word?" mother asked.

"They listen to those that they want to. When I brought this up, he said, 'Why get into all this? There's the issue of caste. You know that the people of that caste are in greater numbers in the village…' and left it at that."

Mother was silent for a while. Then she said, "That's true. Our people being fewer in number is our problem. Even in that small number, we have internal differences… We won't improve." Saying this, she stood up holding the winnow.

"My worry is only about Gorima. She is ill in bed with worry. The older son Saheb has gone and settled in the town. Doesn't bother about the mother. Where is the man who will support her? Everyone asked her to marry again after her husband died. But she carried on somehow, putting her faith in the older son. Thinking of her children all the time… Now she is left all alone. That Anwar is still young…," mother was saying all this as if talking to herself as she went into the kitchen.

Father kept correcting the exam papers in silence. I was thoroughly confused. All I could think of was I had to save Gorima somehow! But how? How? I had no idea.

I could not save Gorima.

But after this, the very nature of our village changed. Soon, mother and father too did not discuss village affairs very much. Father's routine was going on as usual. Mother would sometimes visit Gorima in the afternoons. But she would not talk about it at home. I did not understand anything.

I saw Gorima gradually becoming thin like a skeleton. I saw how Anwarbhai had become a prisoner of the four walls of his room. Also, Gorima moved out of her house with the big rooms to a small hut-like house behind—though I did not know of this change then. Outside, the size of the idol was growing day by day. Earlier, people would come on some Saturdays. Now they were coming every day. I cannot tell you the kind of violence that was taking place there. Under the neem tree with the green and red flags where we used to play, now there were heaps and heaps of cock plumes. Gradually, my attraction towards this place lessened. Even my young eyes could see that Gorima's eyes which had always been filled with love were now filled with a helpless anger and hatred. It was now a situation where no one could do anything anymore. Earlier Gorima would always tell mother that her son Saheb would come and everything would be all right. But I did not see Saheb mamayya again. Except once.

I saw Saheb mamayya when father took me to town with him to buy clothes for Ramzan.

After father bought me a shirt, I made a fuss that I wanted slippers.

"Don't we have a pair at home?"

'No. I want another one."

When I was adamant, father took me to a shoe shop. There, a man saluted father with a sweet smile, and said, "Kya khairiat, saab? How are you, sir?"

There was something both sad and painful in the man's smile and his voice. He was saying something. I was listening to him keenly, thinking there might be some mention of Gorima. But not once, not even inadvertently, did he speak a word about her.

Finally, father said, "Ek baar aao. Come home once. Your mother is all alone. There are a lot of problems."

"Ammee's crazy. When I ask her to come here, she doesn't. As for them, they won't rest until they chase her away. The people of that caste are very shrewd. Stubborn sons of whores. How can we resist them? As for ammee, she speaks high and mighty. Says we must save the house somehow. But we don't have anyone to look up to or turn to for support. We don't have the papers for that site. We can't say or do a thing, saab."

"You come, and you try again."

"I don't have faith, saab. You know how cruel they are. They are thinking of taking over the house somehow and building a big temple there. People from other villages too are supporting them. The other day they came and threatened us. Said that they will do away with us if we don't vacate the house. My children are growing up, saab. I can't pledge my life to this..." Saheb was expressing his helplessness.

Father too was unable to say anything more after this.

"Iska size ek joda nikalo. Take out a pair of slippers his size," he said.

Saheb pulled my feet close to him and took my size.

"Ye log aapko kya dete? What do they give you as salary here?" father asked.

"I am able to get by at present. When the children grow up it will be difficult to manage," Saheb said.

"What has such a big family come to now... In those days how much respect everyone had for Gorey bhai!"

"All that has gone with him. Now except for caste and religion, no one cares about people." Tears shone in Saheb's eyes.

"Come home. Stay for the day and leave," he said affectionately. When he said that, Saheb mamayya looked exactly like Gorima!

"Agle baar zaroor aatey. Next time I will definitely come," father said.

"Bhabhi ko leke aao. Bring sister-in-law along." Saying this, Saheb came out of the shop with us and saw us off.

I cannot tell you how much I irritated father on the return journey with my questions!

"Who was Gorey bhai? Why was Saheb mamayya living away from his mother?"

"Gorey bhai died of malaria. In those days, if one got malaria that was it! As he could not make ends meet, Saheb left the village and came to the town with his wife and children. Insisting that this was their own village and their own home, Gorima stayed back with Anwar," he said in one breath.

But I did not let go. "Now who will look after Gorima?"

"That is how it has to be, babu, until Anwar grows up." Saying this, father lapsed into silence. Nor did he want to say anything more.

A few days after this, Moti pinni came home. Moti pinni was a good friend of Gorima. She was talking to mother and saying, "Aapa. Gorima is waging a huge battle. If she wins this battle, she will get the house. More than the house, their family's honour and prestige will be saved."

"What's the point? She is becoming a corpse. Why fight with the people of that caste? I feel it is better to let that wretched house go," said mother.

"You tell me, aapa, how will she let it go? You know how Gorey bhai and Gorima lived. They were the talk of the village in those days... The house is all that is left of his memory. She wants them to let her have it. Saheb sold the agricultural land they had and went to live in the town."

"But it looks as if along with the house we will also lose Gorima," mother said sadly.

"Allah kya likhe woh hota, aapa, kaun kya karte? What Allah has decreed will happen, sister, what can anyone do?" Saying this, Moti pinni left.

After that, time went by somehow. But Gorima did not keep quiet. She kept fighting. Gradually her house was turning into a temple. Nobody had the power to stop it. Questioning everyone's silence, Gorima continued to protest. As she kept on struggling like that and kept fighting for her home, I was worried what would happen to her. I told mother. I told father. But nobody paid any attention to Gorima. Anwarbhai too stopped coming out of the house. Slowly a distance grew between us.

In the meantime many changes took place. Our family shifted to the town. The little cultivable land that we had in the village was handed over to babai, father's younger brother. Whenever uncle came to visit us in town, he would give us news about the village. That was the only way we knew about what was happening to Gorima—listening to babai.

Lost in all these memories I had finally reached the village. As soon as I entered the village, the police station was on the right as before. But there was such a huge crowd there! In my childhood, barring one or two people, the police station would usually be empty. When I saw the crowd swarming outside, I thought violence in the village must have increased. If you went a little further, there was a grinding mill on the left. It was making a horrendous noise; clearly it hadn't changed much. Stepping thus into the past and the present at the same time, I entered the village. People were going about their way. No one was stopping to look at me or recognising me. When I used to wander about the village as a child, there wasn't one person I did not know, for on seeing me they would always say, "Hindi saar's son!" Today, I felt like a nameless person in that village. Trying to find someone I could recognise among all those strange new faces, I came to the peerla chavidi. Babai's house was four or five steps away from it. A chavidi built in the old style with raised platforms. Its doors would always be open. Except during Muharram, no one took much notice of it. But how much excitement there would be in this chavidi during that month! Saheb mamayya swaying, holding the peer, jumping on hot coals, speaking words as if possessed... for me, a time of intense happiness combined with fear! There was a large vacant space in front of the peerla chavidi. It was there that they would put up a pandal for Sriramanavami. Oh, the excitement of kolatam!

> Siva Siva Murthivi Gananatha, Gananatha you are the image of Siva
> Nuvvu Sivudee Kumarudivi, Gananatha, Gananatha you are the son of Siva

When they would play the kolatam to those rhythmic beats, our feet and hands would move on their own without stopping and we would sway like the peer. As soon as it was evening someone would bring hot pulihora[5] in a large vessel. They would get onto the platform of the peerla chavidi and distribute it to everyone. All those scenes from my childhood were moving so vividly in front of my eyes it was as if I was right there!

When Saheb mamayya and Anwar annayya would sing in the peerla chavidi, they would really weep. Watching them and listening to them sing, even one with a heart of stone would burst out crying.

Still immersed in my memories, I heard a shout, "Babu…!"

I turned to look—it was Usman!

As soon as I saw Usman, I started crying. I embraced him tightly. Without being aware, the words "Usman mama" came out. He too embraced me with the same affection. "You have come after so long, babu," Usman said, wiping his tears.

This Usman had no house or place of his own. He would station himself on this chavidi or that platform for a few days and live like that. How Gorima would get angry with him. "Ye Usman ek deewana! Na ghar ka na ghat ka! This Usman is one crazy good-for-nothing! Doesn't belong anywhere!" she would say. He would always go about adjusting a piece of beedi between his fingers. You would often find him playing with a bunch of children. In fact it was the children who loved to play with him.

Usman said, "Babu mere ghar jayenge. Babu let's go to my house."

Surprised, I asked him, "You have a house?"

"Why? Shouldn't I have a house?"

---

[5]**pulihora:** also pulisoru, puliyogare or puliyodarai, a traditional rice dish made with tamarind, curry leaves and spices, popular across Andhra Pradesh, Telangana, Karnataka, Tamil Nadu and Kerala.

True. My question seemed silly even to me.

"Let me first go and say hello to babai and pinni and then come."

"Bada nikklale! Such a great fellow! Beta has come after such a long time. And that idiot doesn't even think of going to the station to receive you!"

"No, babai doesn't know that I am coming."

"Fine. Come see this poor man's hut first and then go."

But I did not agree. First I had to wish babai. Had to talk to pinni. Had to find out how Mukarram was. I had heard she was not well. I wondered how Jaffer was. All my thoughts centred on them.

Usman seemed to have understood my plight. "All right, I'll come in the evening then after asar namaz," he said.

He walked with me till babai's house. Then, saying, "You go in," he went away. For some reason he did not come in. In my childhood, after the asar namaz late in the afternoon, Usman would forever be hanging around my uncle's place. I felt that something was wrong.

When I went in, babai was not at home. Outside there was a small verandah. At a distance a cattle shed. On hearing my steps someone came out from inside. Mukarram. Tears welled up in my eyes on seeing her. Mukarram looked like a living corpse. Always smiling, chirpy and dancing like a wave...that enthusiasm and happiness—had that girl ever experienced them in her life? Seeing her now, it seemed as if she never had.

"Ammee, Babu bhai is here!" Saying this, she dashed inside the house. Pinni came out. "You have come after so many days, babu. Do you ever think about us, if we are still alive in this village or not? How many problems we are facing! Your mother would never think of us. Neither would you." There was sarcasm in pinni's voice. She hadn't changed one bit, I thought even as I was moving closer to her, and stopped myself right there. Meanwhile Mukarram had brought me a glass of water. As I was about to drink it, pinni started off again, "Do you ever think of our problems, babu?" I put the glass aside and looked at Mukarram. She turned towards me with an affectionate smile, as if to say her mother was just like this.

"Why all this as soon as he comes, ammee? Babu bhai, I'll keep the water for your bath. You have come in the hot sun. You must be tired." Mukarram's words gave me much solace. But even after that, pinni kept on muttering something and grumbling.

"Where is Jaffer?" I asked Mukarram.

"Kaam nai, dhaam nai...ka jaata? No work, nothing to do... where will he go?" pinni cut in. I could see the change in her way of speaking. I knew that our relationship was not what it was before. Mother was perpetually abusing pinni. "Shaadi mejwane mein bhi nai ja saka karee, dushman! She has seen to it that we can't even attend weddings and feasts anymore, the enemy!" Mother would thus speak bitterly of aunt and get furious whenever she was mentioned. But when father would get angry at this, she would go away to do her chores, muttering, "Aa...bhai ke oopar makkhi bhi nai girna! Yes, yes, of course...even a fly mustn't fall on his brother!"

From the beginning father had always had sympathy for babai. "He never studied. As for us, whether it is small or insignificant, I still have a government job," father would say. Whenever he visited them, he would take some grain and vegetables, stay with them for a day or two before returning. Gradually, even those visits became rare. Meanwhile father's health suffered. Expenditure in the house increased. We had to pour out huge sums of money to the hospital. Mother would constantly urge father to go to the village and settle the issue about the land. But father never paid heed. He just kept borrowing money for his illness, and then he passed away. The family was left in debt.

How many times had mother berated me, saying, "You are the eldest son. At least you ought to take interest in the land!" But even if I went to the village, could I ask babai about the land? I had no such faith. I did not have the courage to speak about the land to his face. In fact, I knew his family condition quite well. But unable to refuse mother, I had come. Pinni's sharp, stinging words were words that I had well anticipated. But Mukarram and Jaffer were fond of me from childhood. As for babai, he had neither love for me nor anger. Then, what was I for him?

"Bhai, paani nikaalim. I have kept the water for your bath." These words of Mukarram broke my thoughts.

By the time I had my bath and came out, babai had come.

"Kab aaya, re? When did you come?" he asked me without any emotion on his face. Babai was always like that!

"Just now."

And that was my entire conversation with him. I changed my clothes and came in. Mukarram served food.

"Ek waqt kitne takleefa padthey Allah jane. How many difficulties we have to suffer for just one meal God alone knows," pinni started off again. Mukarram, who was serving me, glared at her mother angrily, that too without her knowledge.

Though I was very hungry I ended the meal without eating much. Perhaps because I had come in the sun, the minute I lay down sleep overpowered me. Even by then Jaffer had not come.

I slept till asar namaz. As I was still lying on the cot, I could hear my aunt's voice from the verandah.

"Why would babu come just like that? He must have come to enquire about the land. Don't mince words but tell him clearly. Tell him that the amount that his father had taken as loan for his treatment is cancelled out in terms of the land value. I had told you then itself that you should have the papers for all that you do…" she was telling uncle. Her words surprised me. Did father take a loan? Did he use up the money on this land without our knowledge? Then what about his other loans in the town? Even if I were to put all those aside, why was pinni speaking so harshly? I shifted restlessly on the cot. Just then Mukarram came in.

"Babu bhai, please don't be upset. How much joy your coming has given us," she said, wiping her tears. Unable to say anything more, she went out. For some reason, I remembered Gorima.

"Deko, o ghar ke vaste Gorima kette jung kareeki! Learn from Gorima, what battles she waged for the sake of that house!" mother would always keep repeating. But we did not know what happened to Gorima in those battles. Now at least I had to find out. But what about my battle? Gorima fought with people of a particular caste. But would I be able to win this battle on the "home front"? Leave that aside, would I be able to take babai to task? I did not have the faith that I would.

Usman came without fail at the time of asar namaz.

"Namazku aao," he insisted. Thinking it would be a relief, I did vazoo and went along with him for namaz.

I was unable to speak a word with Usman on the way. My mind was in turmoil. The only bond I had left with this village was that land of father's...would that too snap? If I didn't speak out now, I would never have the opportunity of speaking up again. Perhaps I would never be in a position to come to this village again! Pinni would cause as much obstruction as she could. She would not let babai come in her way. Mukarram's sorrowful face; bava, my brother-in-law, forever tormenting Mukarram for his jode ka rakam;[6] Jaffer unsettled without a job; mother who was constantly questioning my incompetence; brothers who always expectantly looked to me to bring back something to relieve the burden of father's loans...Ya Allah!

"Parvardigare Aalam, O sustainer of grief...," Usman sighed as if voicing my unspoken thoughts. Did he know my inner turmoil?

I was thinking of all this as I climbed the steps and entered the masjid. As soon as I stepped into that tranquil environment, my mind felt calmer. Hazrat Saab looked towards me. I bent down, saluted him and buried my head in his lap. He affectionately pulled me close to him and, squinting his old eyes as he peered into my face, asked, "Kaun, beta? Who are you, my child?"

"Hamare Munwar aapa ka beta, bhool gaye?! He's our Munwar aapa's son. Don't you recall?" Usman said, as the old man tried to recollect. Everyone in the village knew me only as Munwar aapa's son. After namaz I did dua to Allah and prayed—that our relationship with babai's family be strengthened; that Mukarram's relationship with her husband be set right. For a while I sat silently in the masjid. I thought it was best not to quarrel with babai over the land. No matter what mother said, I thought I would get a loan or some such and set right the affairs of the family there itself. Having decided thus, I felt very calm and at peace.

---

[6]**jode ka rakam:** gift of money given to the bridegroom by the bride's side to buy clothes.

When we came outside, Usman insisted that we go to his house. I agreed. We were walking along when he suddenly said, "Zameen chhodo nakko... Abba ki yaad hai na. Don't let go of the land... It is all that is left of your father's memory."

Usman's words once more disturbed the calm that had encircled me within. Yes, it was father's memory... If Usman was so persistent, how persistent would amma be? I was once again lost in thought. Nanna's smile caressed me like a cool breeze wafting over a green field. How many sorrows had that smile hidden...! I was torn and sobbing inside, but outwardly I was unable to utter a word. Yes, that land was indeed nanna's memory. I must not let it go. My entire body was clenched like a fist.

"Don't look at your uncle's face and think of letting it all go, babu. If you ask me there is no greater non-believer or demon than that uncle of yours."

"How come I didn't see Gorima?" I asked Usman.

When I heard what Usman had to say, my eyes filled with tears. He left, saying he would return to fetch me in time for me to take the train back to town.

By the time Usman came, I had packed my bag and was ready. Saying "Khuda hafiz," I took leave of babai's family, and set out for the station with Usman.

When we had walked some distance, Usman himself brought up the topic. "What have you decided about the land, babu?"

I did not reply.

Soon we reached the station. The same familiar scene of people and bustle.

The old burkha-clad beggar woman was there. As soon as she saw Usman, she spoke to him.

"Gorima!" I said aloud.

She looked into my eyes. "Akbar...?"

She did not have the strength even to get up. Sitting on the ground she caressed me with affection from head to foot. I stretched out both my hands to her and she clasped them in hers, her eyes brimming with tears.

"See, this is what I have finally come to, babu! There is nothing left. I have drowned."

"What happened? How did all this happen?"

But she was unable to speak a word more. Usman intervened and began to tell me her story. After listening to everything, Gorima appeared to me to stand as tall as the sky and I wanted to bow down and touch her feet. Tears flowed freely down my face. Her protest, her rightful struggle for her home, her land... Before Gorima, I was nothing but a dwarf!

Just then the loud noise of the train pulling into the platform snapped me out of my thoughts.

Usman ran ahead and found a seat for me. As I slumped onto my seat, I kept looking at Gorima.

Gorima, you are the history that this country cannot write. You are the revolution. You are the struggle that our generation does not know and cannot understand. You have fought a lone battle against all of society for the sake of your land. Even in defeat, you have in truth won. You have your feet still planted firmly on the ground. As for me, I am running away like a coward, far away from this land...

When I looked up out of the window, I saw a swarm of white clouds rushing across the sky, like the war horses raging in Gorima's heart.

Originally published in Telugu as 'Gorima'
in *Aadivaram Vartha*, 29 December 2002; and
in *Katha* (2002), pp. 23–42.

2. Mustafa's Death

"Don't peep into this room, beta!" I could hear Fatima phupma's voice loud and clear—from such a long time ago.

From the time that Muneer bhai had called three days ago to say, "We are doing the tenth day rites for abbajaan," I don't know how many times I had heard that shout from the past.

If I were to take the bus very early today, and reach the village by afternoon, I would be there for the tenth day rites. Thinking it would be good to spend some time with Muneer bhai, Fatima phupma and Gorima, I set out for the village. I need to talk, and talk a lot, especially about that room.

What will happen to that room now that Muneer bhai's father Mustafa is no more? Will Muneer bhai take over that room and that tradition as an heirloom? What will Muneer bhai, who had shouldered all the responsibility even when his father was alive, do now? What will happen to all the hundreds of devotees who had followed Mustafa's way?

There are so many questions. But all my questions begin and end with that room.

Mustafa's life was a difficult one that turned so many hues even as one watched it go by. A scene from it would appear to be different at different moments in time and in different situations to an observer. How could any one colour then truly capture Mustafa's whole life? To me it was a medley of colours impossible to describe.

But didn't the whole village believe that Baba Mustafa had no death? They had come to such a philosophical state of blind belief. Listening to his stories, mesmerised by his words, listening to all the fantastic tales narrated by the villagers, which had then spread to the neighbouring villages, even I had pushed myself into a state where I too had started believing, "Yes, perhaps it was true: death won't even come close to Mustafa."

The whole village was convinced that if a deluge came in the form of a gigantic tidal wave, Baba Mustafa would dance on the head of that wave, and if it came in the form of fire, he would play with it! For the Muslims of the village, my paternal aunt Fatima's husband Mustafa—and the father of Muneer, Munaf, Mumtaz, Momeen and Mahmooda, who I used to play with—was a Maulana. In the words of Gorima, whom I adored, "He has Deeni malumaat: true knowledge of Islam. He is one who has truly understood the meaning of devotion."

But in the end, Mustafa did not retain any of these positions. He flung them all away and he disappeared—into the dark room.

When Muneer said that his abba had passed away, I was in a quandary: should I or should I not go? Even if I went, would I be able to bear to see Muneer's family, which was just like my own, in that state?

Muneer is my best friend. Our houses in the village were a little far apart but we would spend most of the day together. As we were in the same class we would also study together. People would sometimes ask us jokingly and sometimes vengefully, "Are you two twins?" Even after I left the village, there was no change in our friendship. The only difference now is that there isn't much exchange of news between us anymore, that's all.

One evening, when I was sitting on the edge of the platform in front of Mustafa's room, and slowly parting the white curtain to peer behind it, Momeen saw me and immediately called out, "Ammee! Apu bhai is going inside abbajaan's room!" Fatima phupma who was somewhere inside the house came out running, pulled me away and pleaded, "No ra, babu, no! If mamayya sees, he will kill you!"

But the thing is, there really were no prohibitions or restrictions for me in their house. So whenever I was told such things, I felt very strange. In fact it only made me more curious to know.

We were only just beginning to understand the outside world. We were beginning to understand why Mustafa became a Maulana. And as we watched, we saw Mustafa transferring himself completely into that room, and that room becoming his beginning and end.

It was at that juncture that Gorima began our Quran lessons. It was the unwritten custom in our families that by the time we were eleven we ought to have completed learning the Quran. The Arabic primer *Alif, Lam, Meem* had been completed. "Bacche, come home this Friday after namaz. I will read the Jaggery Fateha[1] and start the Quran Shareef for you," Gorima said. With this pronouncement, there was a new excitement in my heart.

After I had read the first Arabic book, Arabic became ginger murabba to me. Oh, and I must also tell you a story about this ginger murabba—if we did not eat Meera Sayibu's ginger murabba before morning tea, we felt as if it had not dawned! Even before we had started reading the Quran, Gorima made us memorise a few of the Quran suras. Once we had learnt them by heart, these suras would roll out as smoothly from our tongue as the Arabic murabbas. Every Friday it was wonderful to hear the Arabic sentences unfurl from the mouth of the Maulana during namaz. On Jagne ki Raat we would stay up all night in the masjid just to listen to Mustafa's sonorous voice rolling out each Arabic letter, syllable and word.

But all this soon changed. Mustafa's voice changed. His manner changed. It appeared almost as if a new person emerged from his body. In the new world Mustafa created outside the masjid, we found no place, including in the room.

"It is good not to enter that room, ra! Your sobat, your bond is only with the Allah above, and not with the shaitan that has squatted here." When Gorima made it a point to tell us this time

---

[1]**Jaggery Fateha:** devotees offer jaggery or sugar in return for their vow, and the Muslim caretaker of the peerla chavidi or pir house recites the first verse of the Quran, Al Fateha, over the sacred food before distributing it to them.

and again, we decided that we had to enter that room, the four or five of us.

What was there in that room? This and this alone was our search then and our constant anxiety.

To search for the secrets hidden in that room, we traversed all the imaginary universes that our young minds could imagine. If we pushed aside that white curtain and entered, what would we see? Every night Fatima phupma would rub and wash the white curtain clean, and hang it back on the door again in the morning.

"Why phupma?" I would ask her almost daily.

"It's just become an idiosyncrasy, babu. If the shaitan comes and sits on your head, then the whole world will look crooked to you. That is how your mamayya's business also seems to be," she would say.

Though Muneer was two or three years older than me, he too did not really understand what that business was all about. But I could feel a sense of distaste in his words. Things became such that each of us held his own views on the matter.

As to how much our thoughts revolved around that room, for a long time we would see it in our dreams. We would dream that Mustafa himself took us into that room and showed us strange, some very strange things, that we were listening to him with our eyes wide open, that we were touching and feeling each and every object in that incredible world. We would share those dreams with each other. After listening to all of it, Muneer bhai would say, "You have really become obsessed with it. Actually, there is nothing at all in that room, ra."

"Have you ever looked inside?"

"No...abba does not allow anyone to go in."

"Then how do you know?"

"I *don't* know! I don't even *want* to know!" Muneer would say and go away.

The first time I asked Gorima about this, she said, "Mustafa is screaming with too much knowledge, ra. He is living in illusion, craving more and still more powers and desires. Allah will never forgive such things." She made us memorise the Al Bakra suras in the Quran that day. But what was exceptional about Gorima is that she wouldn't just ask us to memorise them blindly. She would also explain their meanings to us in great detail. But we still believed that there was a wonderful world inside that room, way beyond all her explanations.

We began to feel that there was a secret treasure that we did not know of and that we could not know or understand. Muneer bhai, who had just begun to understand the world, seemed to know a little about those things, but he never spoke about them.

Before we could break out of our obsessive curiosity and anxiety, Mustafa's house turned into a pilgrim centre. What started as a crowd of tens soon reached the hundreds. Some devotees built a small room a few feet away from where Muneer's family lived. Early one morning, before we had even woken up, all of Mustafa Baba's paraphernalia was shifted into that room. On a tree in front of the newly constructed room, a green flag began to flutter.

"What wretched times!" I saw Fatima phupma beating her head and cheeks as she was saying this. "Mustafa himself does not know what he is doing," said Gorima, before lapsing into silence, as if it was unnecessary to say anything more whenever the topic of Mustafa was raised.

But there was no place for silence within me. A great unease, as if a restless ocean was roaring inside, as if a host of dark clouds were turning rapidly into a downpour. An inexplicable consuming fear as if something that ought not to happen was happening, as if it was drowning the whole village like a gigantic tidal wave.

Even as all these were happening, my father was transferred to another village. We reached a town that was close to the village. After that, the village was just a memory. Muneer was just a childhood friend. But that room remained in a corner of my mind. The white curtain that hung on the door of that room and the large green flag on the tree in front of the room did not stop fluttering before my eyes.

I would come to know about Mustafa Baba only through the words of some people. Sometimes Muneer would call. He would give me all the news of the village—except about his father. I had observed that he wanted to gradually erase the mention of his father even when I was in the village. So his not mentioning his father at all after we came to town appeared quite natural to me. In Muneer's view, that room was an enemy. A dark cave. Be it ignorance or excess of knowledge, it was a tangled circle.

By the way, what would Mustafa do in that room? One thing was for certain—that room alone was the space between his outer and inner worlds. He did not have a home, family, responsibility or masjid. Had no wife or children. Except for the devotees who came for him. Except for the rituals and prayers they performed. Except for the conversation he had with God for their sake in that room.

Each time, after listening to his devotees' pleas and requests, Mustafa would go inside the room for half an hour and come out. During that time all kinds of stories of karamat, exceptional miraculous powers about Mustafa Baba would overpower the devotees.

At a time when the bhajans and prayers for Mustafa were increasing, Gorima warned him countless times, saying, "Mustafa, you won't have even a word left to answer God in your final moments. What you are doing is wrong. No one has said this in Islam of any kind. You are harbouring boundless greed."

Would Mustafa listen! But one good thing was that Mustafa was not a greedy man. He believed that what he was doing was spiritually proper and holy. This was in another way a loss to the family. After Mustafa transformed into a Baba the entire responsibility of the family fell on Muneer bhai's head. Unable to bear the burden of such a big family, he was distraught. It came to a stage when the entire family detested the path Mustafa had taken. "Truly, what does ibaadat or devotion even mean to you? Is it to make your family completely destitute?" Gorima tried thus to reason with Mustafa umpteen number of times. But each time

Mustafa would withdraw into his room, saying, "For all times, Gorima, this is my way. Let me go my way."

Before he had disappeared into that room Mustafa would do namaz five times a day. The black mark on his forehead seemed like God's signature for his dedication.

During the month of Ramzan we would look forward to Mustafa's sermon. In his voice, the suras of Quran would sound pleasing to the ears. We would wonder what kind of life it would be if one did not read the Quran. Gorima too had respect for the Mustafa of those days. As for the village, there was no refuting his words. During those days Mustafa fell into deep spiritual contemplation, and started living often unmindful of time. That situation came to stay.

It is difficult to understand Muneer bhai in the brief conversation we have over the phone. I am worried as to how Muneer bhai has taken his father's demise. This worry too was just like the worry about Mustafa's room!

By the time I get down from the bus, Muneer is waiting for me at the bus stand.

I do not know what to say. The truth of the matter is that it is the room that has taken over my mind entirely.

"Let's have tea here and then go," Muneer says.

At the tea shop near the bus stand, Raju recognises me and asks, "How are you, saaru?"

"Fine," I say as I take the tea from him, and both of us sip the tea, standing under a tree next to the tea shop. As we are sipping tea, Muneer asks me about the affairs of our house and listens, but he does not say anything about the affairs of his home. I too do not feel like asking him immediately. I think I can ask him as we walk along.

Muneer has always been a quiet person. Looking at him, I understand that he has become even quieter. His face is so pinched that he looks exhausted. Half his hair has greyed. His body looks weak. Muneer is an example of one who has failed in so many ways. I feel that Muneer's back has been really bent taking the burden of his family.

By the time I think of bringing up the topic of Mustafa's death, we reach his house. Fatima phupma, Muneer's brothers and sisters are happy to see me.

Gorima too is there. Seeing me, she pulls me close and caresses my head. Seeing Gorima after such a long time makes me happy too. The same tranquility in her face.

As I sit in the verandah, my eyes search everywhere for Mustafa's room.

After all the rituals of the tenth day are over in the afternoon, after the few relatives leave, Muneer dozes in the chair for a while. I keep looking at his face. There is disquiet in him. There is sorrow. There is also a trace of relief. Sometimes Muneer seems like a Karbala warrior to me. In that battle, at least a few people survived. But in this Karbala battlefield, he always seems to be the lone warrior. How many battles add up to a life! Spirituality may be great peace, but it can also be a great battle.

As for life, it is the chaos of so many battles! Did Mustafa immerse himself in the battle of spirituality because he was unable to fight the many battles of life? Perhaps. I do not know Mustafa's battle. Muneer too does not know. When I had asked Gorima once, she had explained it in just one sentence: "Spirituality is like an open space. The end of the earth ought to be visible. The sky above and the land below should be visible. That is all, but it must not become a constricted space." Is that so? Allah said seven skies, but has He said seven lands anywhere? I do not know. I do not know so many things.

Mustafa created an easy heaven for the people here. Thinking that that little bit of heaven was enough, people imagined that God in Mustafa. But for his own people, Mustafa became a demon! How...? How to fathom this difference? Just then, snapping me out of my thoughts, Muneer opens his eyes and asks me, "Shall we go out for a bit?"

"Why don't you have some tea before you go," says Fatima phupma. Even before we say yes, she places two glasses in front of us.

Her eyes are always two peaceful rivers. If you hurl a stone into that river, that river will pull it into its stomach. You can't see even a tiny ripple. Her pure, unostentatious eyes accept any situation with single-minded disinterestedness.

How was she when the body of the husband she had lived with for so many years and who had fathered so many children turned cold? Did she like everyone cry as if her heart was breaking, banging her fists on the ground? It might not have happened like that. Did she sit crouched in a corner like a light put out? I do not know...I cannot imagine even that.

After having his tea, Muneer says, "Come, let's go."

"Muneer bhai, I've been meaning to ask you, but restrained myself thinking that you might misunderstand. Haven't you told the people outside about abba's death?"

"Our village knows. Other villages don't know. We did not tell them on purpose."

"Why?"

"We don't want all that fuss. You know that ammee, Gorima and I have kept a distance from all this."

"Yes, I know. Phupma never agreed with this path."

"If you ask me, this is not even a path. It's a turn in the path. God is a veil. Devotion is a lure!"

"I understand. But...after the man has gone, isn't all this unnecessary?"

"I don't know... All this has created a great intolerance in all of us. A fire that has emerged out of years of burning embers. A state when we can no longer bear it."

I do not feel like making him say anything more than this. It is not as if I do not know what they are all going through!

"But, that room...?"

"Would you like to see it? Come, I'll show you." Saying this, Muneer bhai took me to the place where the room and the tree with the flag were. The minute we reached the spot I saw that the room was no longer there. But thinking I might have made a mistake I did not say anything.

"This is where it was," Muneer says. "There is not even a trace of it now to show that there used to be a room here. Everything is flat. We broke it down. The very next day after abba died."

"So soon?"

"Yes. We did not want to continue with it. We thought it best for the world and for us to end the story right there," Muneer says without hesitation.

I sit on a stone right there and imagine for a while that the room is still there. The room that has haunted me from childhood has remained a thing of imagination even now. I can sense Mustafa's shadow moving around that invisible room.

"Okay...let's go now," Muneer says very casually, aware that the room is still very much on my mind, but ignoring it.

"That room is always a dark cave for me. I strongly believe that God exists. No matter who tells me, I will not believe that God is there in these dark rooms or in strange powers or in caves. When I broke it down, I was liberated from that darkness," he says as we come out.

"Has this story then ended this way?" I meant to mutter to myself, but the words just came out.

"Yes, we ourselves have to force an ending to some stories." These words of Muneer do not allow me to sleep that day.

Originally published in Telugu as 'Mustafa Maranam'
in *Andhra Jyothy*, 29 January 2012; and in *Katha* (2012), pp. 43–52.

3. Sahil Will Come

A few pages in the diary...disturbed sleep. These four or five nights, I alone walking around Charminar, and I going around myself, no one else about—just the lone Charminar with the four hands aloft.

A dream that haunts me in my half asleep state—Charminar.

In the broken dream, corpses of kaleidoscopes of butterflies.

I can hear the sound of my footsteps over them. I am listening.

Exactly a week ago, Sahil, Phani and I had roamed about here like children with the enthusiasm of the colours of butterflies, swaying rhythmically, with our hands firmly on each others' shoulders.

Now that's a memory!

Sahil would sing.

There would be a butterfly in that singing note, with the same urge, the same verve. Wonder which innocent jasmine hands will save it from becoming another corpse!

Wonder with which pure words of a tender voice would it rise from the dead again and again!

Sometimes...No, no, many a time.

That butterfly is me...it is really me!

Sometimes, it is also you.

These are not my sentences alone. Some of these are what I heard in Urdu from Sahil's mouth. In the state in which I am now, turning those sentences this way and that I am trying to understand my frame of mind.

Butterfly in Sahil's language is...titli!

But in my world, Titli is not just a butterfly—she is my language, my world, my little one...everything.

I have to tell everything to my Titli.

Titli too has to tell me everything.

On a day that we don't tell each other everything like this, it doesn't get dark for us.

Our eyes won't close. Even if they do, we can't fall asleep. Even if we sleep, it is disturbed sleep.

Each night, after dinner our house turns into slow motion. The three of us pass into another stage between wakefulness and sleep. Neeru rearranges the kitchen one more time. As for me, I go straight to bed, tired.

Then, Titli would arrive—just like her name—on her butterfly wings!

Today too, I ate my meal. As if one had to do it somehow. While eating I exchanged a few words with Neeru. As if that too was unavoidable.

When I was doing all this indifferently, Titli noticed it all. I knew. Even now I know that I cannot tell Titli all that I know.

I also know that Titli has been keenly observing me for the past two days.

She is as fond of Sahil as I am of him. Isn't it he who gave her that pet name! "Only that this little one doesn't have wings; if a butterfly were born like a baby, it would be just like this!" Saying this, Sahil named her Titli. Once he had named her so, it was so strongly entrenched in our minds that most of the time we would not remember that she had another name.

She would play with Sahil, sing with him. She would tell him all kinds of things for hours together. To say it in a word, when the two of them are together, they become the same age. Though Sahil had crossed thirty, there was a shade of childhood in him still. I am very fond of that childlike quality in him!

I have to tell Titli everything.

Titli too has to tell me everything.

Today too, Titli came and stood in front of me like a mirror.

In that mirror I must see myself having gone back into that innocent childhood!

Everything...I must reveal everything. Must open up without minding the layers of the mind. No word must remain unspoken. Must not remain unspoken even once.

But at that moment I could not speak. Not a word was coming out. What should I tell this innocent eight-year-old called Titli? What should I tell my little one who thinks that the world is a pure flower that blossoms? Could I point out to even one inner thought and say definitely that this is "it"? Unable to say it, should I tell her a few cock and bull stories, sweet gossip and make her go to sleep?

What shall I say, Titli? What shall I say? The Sahil you and I know is a Sahil the world is newly unravelling...Not one, but Sahil is now two...two, it seems!

I slipped into my silence. I kept telling Titli something or the other in that silence.

Sahil is singing from somewhere.

> No matter how much I tell you, you don't know what kind
> of a world this is.
> It wipes away the rainbow on the wings of a butterfly.
> It sculpts strange artificial colours.
> Smearing the western dusk with blood it calls it bloodshed.
> Suspicions, shame, doubts, questions all over its body.

"Wipe it clean!" I wanted to say this aloud in so many contexts, but am unable to wipe away the conversation that took place this morning in the police station, like spit on the face or mud on the shirt.

"One must leave certain things just as they are! Must forget them! Work is important for us!" Phani is saying.

"Isn't that why I kept quiet? Otherwise my blood was boiling. Even if I were to forget, won't Haseena remember it always? That means by now she must have experienced the shame and suspicion that underlie the label 'Muslim'! Will you disagree?"

I have no answer to Phani's question.

Don't know where Sahil has gone!

It would have been good if he had come back this morning…I had thought to myself twenty-five or thirty times and a dozen times aloud. But in this city where it was not certain whether the man who left the house in the morning would come back intact in the evening…where religion remained a cause for enmity in everyday violence…unable to contain my anguish, I had climbed the steps of the police station. By then there wasn't a place where Haseena with her relatives and we with our friends had not searched. There was no trace of him anywhere. Even if I had gone to the police station, I should not have looked at that Circle Inspector's face. Or it would have been good if someone else had been on duty that morning instead of him.

Even without listening to us, the Circle Inspector said, "Sahil… that means a Muslim—isn't that so? Mohammad? Or a Sheikh? Or a Syed?" Sarcasm in that tone.

Phani looked at my face doubtfully. "Isn't his family name Mohammad?"

"Don't know. I only know his name, Sahil." Saying this I turned towards Haseena. By then she was petrified. The fear of climbing the steps of the police station for the first time was evident in her eyes. She collected herself with some effort and slowly said, "Mohammad."

The Circle Inspector turned towards us and said, "Whether it is Mohammad or Syed, he's a Muslim, right? Since when have you known him?"

"From junior college," Phani and I replied at the same time.

"Did you know him really well? I mean were you close? In the language of Muslims, jigri, best friends?" Again that scathing sarcasm in the Circle Inspector's voice. I felt a sharp knife twisting inside me. "Yes," I said. This time too the two of us spoke as if in unison.

The Circle Inspector looked somewhat pitifully at us. As if that friendship was against the law.

"I must tell you something. He is a Muslim, you are Hindus. His is a Muslim mind! A Muslim mind means violence. It is not all that easy to understand—quite a mystery! He may have led a life you aren't even aware of. Even after so many bomb blasts, bus burnings, deaths and murders, if you don't understand this much, you must either be very naïve or trapped in some strange delusion."

"Impossible!" I felt like shouting, thumping the desk with my fist. As if Phani had read my mind, he looked into my eyes as if to say, keep quiet for a while.

True, both Phani and I know Sahil—as a husband to a wife who he wanted should lead a normal life like everyone else; a father to a sweet ten-year-old who was their dream child; a small-time employee who felt it was enough if the day passed by without event. More than this, as a friend who could give his life for his friends and for our friendship. What more could we say about Sahil?! A man who would give his life for good music; who could capture the beauty of the ghazal in every sentence he spoke—these were the two constants in his life which formed the basis of the beautiful bridge he built between him and his friends.

Above all, above all else, there was an unbreakable bond between our two families, since God knows when. A closeness that made Sahil a pillar of support at each festival, at each family function.

Isn't it because of that conviction that Haseena came running, bringing her son with her, even though it was so late at night?

I had never seen tears in Haseena's eyes.

For that matter, it was the first time I had seen Haseena so late at eleven o'clock in the night.

After dinner, when we were thinking of going to bed, Haseena suddenly knocked on the door. Her eyes filled with tears. A trembling body. Next to her, her son—ten-year-old Faiz—too was in the same state.

"Sahil isn't back home yet!" Haseena said anxiously.

Neeru asked them to come in first and sit down.

Both of them collapsed on the sofa. "Bolo...Haseena!" said Neeru, warmly pulling Haseena's hands close.

Haseena was a strong person. She would not worry unnecessarily.

She would be smiling, making others smile, bright like the sprightly flow of water. In Sahil's words, "Perhaps even its flow could be quiet for a while, but we can't keep Haseena quiet. Haseena's is the language of lively laughter. Even if the other person did not know Urdu, language would not inhibit her laughter." If one were to speak to Haseena for a while, even mounds of worry would melt down just like that. That's why Neeru is very fond of Haseena, Sahil's life! Needless to say what Titli feels.

"He isn't back since morning, Ramu bhai!" Haseena said, crying.

She was unable to stop weeping. That was a Sunday. Sahil would not go to work. On Sundays he would come out for an hour and a half with us—that is us, the crazy trio—to Chai Mahal and have tea, but he wouldn't go anywhere else.

Phani was the first one to notice that Sahil had not come that evening. As we kept saying, "He will come, he will surely come," our hour-and-a half went by. After drinking two cups of tea, each of us went back to our homes. It would have been good perhaps if at least I had walked a few steps and gone to Sahil's house.

Seeing Haseena weep, and Faiz's worried eyes, I now felt guilty that I had made a grave mistake.

"Bhabhi! Stay the night here. He must be caught somewhere in the traffic. Don't worry." As I was saying this I was thinking, but... Sahil not coming back home this late at night...Why? I too did not have an answer to this question. "Call Phani, please," said Neeru. I called Phani immediately. No response. He must have been asleep.

By the time I decided to call him again, Phani called back. I gave him the information. But, he too didn't know what to do. He thought from many different angles, and finally said, "Arey, let's wait till morning. If he doesn't turn up, my friend Circle Inspector Sunil is there, right...let's go to him." I could hear the note of helplessness and anxiety in his tone.

How could I not know about Sahilgadu's whereabouts? There were no secrets between us. Don't know how much I confided in him, but Sahil had the habit since our junior college days of telling me everything in detail, like one threading a bead.

He would not be at peace if he did not rush to our house—in truth, to Titli—every evening, after returning from office and spending a quarter of an hour with Haseena and his son.

But today…Sahil?

I can say with a full heart that I know everything about Sahil. There may not be adequate opportunities to find out what is there in common between the two of us; but if, in those rare situations and moments when one's innermost and basic instincts are awakened, one finds companionship, such companionship is indeed good. It is a lasting companionship.

Sahil came to my room one summer afternoon, during our undergraduate days. I had just got up from a snooze and was sitting, holding a tea cup.

As soon as he had come, he bent his head shyly and said, "Arey Ramu, I have been doing something wrong…since a week."

"A wrong…?"

"Yes. You know Haseena, right?"

"Yes, I know. How can I not know?" I had said, mischievously looking into his eyes. He knew that in that age, there were no secrets that the eyes of very close friends could miss. I had discerned the truth of the language of his eyes much before he himself did. But then thinking, why should I spell it out before he told me, I had kept quiet like a chhupa rustam, one who knows but feigns innocence.

"It is true that I am head over heels in love with Haseena, but the things that I see in my dreams, in my sleep are not good," he had said, his head still bowed.

I had immediately understood what he meant. In fact, there had been no need for him to even say anything to me. But his was a state where he could not but say it.

"If I were to conceal anything from you, I won't be able to sleep the whole night," Sahil had said.

"So you want to spoil our sleep too, bewakoof! Though we have come of age, Phani and I are ashamed that we are still unable to attract a girl!" I had said.

"My love for Haseena is a beautiful accident. Like the flow of a ghazal. This whole world is just the two; that the two are one is like the excitement of a mehfil, a performance! But this wretched body and these dreams surrounding it are throwing me into a trap. I fear that I may commit some wrong!"

"Even if you were to fall into a trap, Haseena will never let you succumb to it. As for your dreams, you must bear with them! Don't be frightened by all the jayaz-najayaz, moral-immoral injunctions of Islam. Dream...dream as much as you can. After marriage, busy with children, responsibilities, you may not have the time to dream!"

But Sahil had not remained dreaming for too long. A feeling that he was doing something gravely wrong—something wrong according to Islam—had not let him remain like that. Even before he had completed his degree, he joined work as a manager in a footwear shop in order to settle down financially, just so that he could marry Haseena. Such was his determination concerning morals and ethics!

I remember clearly, as does Phani, the words Sahil had spoken a week before taking that decision. "I cannot do anything that is not proper and right. Even though it may be confined only to my body!"

"You still belong to the bygone age of truth!" I had said, and still remember the jokes that Phani and I had cracked right on his face.

When I think of it now, I wonder if there was a dilemma within Sahil all the time. I don't know. But I know one thing is true for sure—Sahil can never do anything that would harm another. For that matter, he is a weak person. What did that Circle Inspector say: "The Muslim mind behind the bomb blast—was it Sahil's?"

I have to tell Titli everything. But how to tell her this now?

Will I be able to tell her? Will I be able to tell her all the lies that keep piling up around Sahil, all the stories behind them?

Will I be able to see the Sahil who I have known all these days and the Sahil who has disappeared today as separate? Even the world will soon know that these are all fabricated stories. If Sahil doesn't turn up by tomorrow, then I cannot but laugh at all my questions and doubts!

That evening, Phani said that we could have a cup of tea as usual at Chai Mahal. But I find the thought of tea and Chai Mahal without Sahil distasteful.

"Even before a drop of tea slides down the throat, taste a ghazal samosa!" Saying this, he would recite two consecutive ghazals. Here's the one I liked best between them.

> She knows what love is but my beautiful beloved doesn't know my house.
> Perhaps she had heard the name of God but she doesn't know His whereabouts.
> Perhaps I was distracted, I don't know when youth breezed in or where it went.
> I know spring came and stood outside the door, but I don't know when it became fall.

How scintillating this ghazal sounds in his voice one cannot envision until one hears him recite! Sahil's presence is like sitting in a full mehfil listening to a live contest between music on the one hand and song on the other!

Is Sahil becoming just a memory today?

No, no...it cannot be...No, not at all.

Phani is saying something. But I am unable to hear anything. Some song is enveloping the Mahal like waves. But not a single wave of that song is touching me.

Even before the tea comes, I get up from there and leave.

That mehfil without Sahil...I felt I don't need it at all.

As soon as I come home, Neeru sees me, and she quickly brings tea. She is about to turn on the TV. But I say no. She keeps quiet.

"No...!" I say, and I go to the next room and lie down on my bed without changing my clothes.

Neeru follows me into the room.

"Haseena came today, bringing Faiz with her," she says.

"Is that so?"

"Yes. I'm very worried looking at Haseena. Faiz and Titli played for a while. But Faiz was not in a playful mood. They stayed for a while and went back."

"What shall we do, Neeru? I don't know what to do."

"If you don't mind, can I ask you something? Perhaps what you heard in the police station is true. Perhaps there is a side to Sahil that we don't know..." she says very softly.

I turn impatiently to look at Neeru's face. Unable to bear my stern gaze, Neeru looks down.

"I say this because, if you consider this from another angle, you can search for Sahil," she says even more softly.

"Please...don't say anything anymore...just leave me alone for a while," I say sharply, and turn aside.

What I mean to say is that having another angle is not wrong. But what I also want to say is that Sahil is not the kind of person to behave in that manner without our knowledge. Has Neeru not understood this? And, after all this time, for Neeru to see Sahil only as a Muslim now...?!

"You cannot give explanations to anyone. Now everyone looks at Sahil only as a Muslim, but no one thinks that a human being has gone missing. That's the way it is now." I remember Phani's remark.

Does Titli too wonder who Sahil is?

Titli enters the room just then.

"Nanna!" she says, and comes and lies down next to me.

"Nanna, Faiz came today, but he didn't stay long."

"Is that so?" I say, drawing her close.

"Nanna, Sahil mamu..." She is about to say something more.

I look into Titli's eyes. The same innocent eyes. A bit of wetness beneath their sparkle.

"Nanna, Sahil mamu will come…he will play with us." Saying this, Titli embraces me.

I cannot control my tears.

Hugging Titli, I keep crying.

Originally published in Telugu as 'Sahil Vastadu'
in *Aadivaram Andhra Jyothy*; and
in *Randhi-2013, Telangana Kathala Sankalam*, pp. 53–63.

4. The Chamki-Flowered Horse

"Now that horse...that chamki-flowered horse, a horse with glittering gold pieces...I am getting really angry with the doll! Isn't it because of this doll that I am not in a position to talk with Munnee?"

"Go...go away, you...Chamki!"

Saying this aloud, Apoo throws the doll in her hand on the bed. You know how delicately she threw the doll...With fear in her heart that something might happen to it, she threw it as gently and as softly as possible.

After she throws it, she is unable to think and murmurs, "Let it be, you wretched Chamki." Then she runs up to the bed, eagerly takes the doll in her hands and caresses it lovingly with her soft fingers, anxiously wondering if it has been hurt or pained.

How Apoo adores this horse of chamkis! On the tender mango-leaf coloured horse, a black mane. On its back a velvet cloth, shining red makhmal, with glittering chamkis stitched on it. When she is sliding slowly into sleep at night, after all the lights are turned off, how wonderfully they shine! In those tiny glitters, Apoo shares many things with Chamki.

As to why she adores that horse...you know how lovingly Munnee had given it to Apoo! Also because Munnee is very very dear to Apoo! To say it in the language of Munnee's mother, it is because Munnee and Apoo are both "jigar ka tukda," a part of the same heart!

When Apoo is away from Munnee, she draws Chamki close, embraces it, and calls it over and over again, lovingly, affectionately, "Munnee!" Apoo tells Chamki all the news she wishes to tell Munnee. Even when she is in her mother's lap, looking at the sky through the window, Apoo is showing the stars in the sky to Chamki, and counting them, she slides into sleep.

It is now five days today—five days of Apoo not seeing Munnee, Apoo not playing with Munnee.

There are no stories, no news shared with Munnee. She can't go to Munnee's house and create mischief sitting in front of her grandmother, Fatamma. She can't say "oo" in response to Fatamma who keeps telling them stories.

On the first peer festival[1] evening that Apoo attended after she became aware of the world, it was Fatamma who narrated the very first peer story to her. Till then Apoo thought that peer only meant a doll in the shape of a hand. But after listening to Fatamma's story she understood that peers were not mere dolls, they were great people like gods. That was why all the people in the village prayed to them so devotedly.

"Yes, would people become gods just like that!" Saying this, her mother too told her the very same story that Fatamma had told her. There is a story that when there was famine in the village, it was the peer god who got rid of it. And when some big crowds waged a war on the village, that the peer god took up the sword and pierced through the crowd, and that he staked his life and rescued the village is another story. There is another big story that is sung in the peerla chavidi that in the final war the enemy plotted and killed the peer god on the battlefield.

But all that aside, how wonderfully Fatamma makes palakhova![2] What is Fatamma doing right now with the piece of palakhova that she would hide just for her! Would Munnee eat it up without her? Or, will she hide all of them and give them to her when they meet?

---

[1]**peer festival:** (in Telugu) Peerla Panduga is another name for Muharram as observed by Muslims in Telangana and Andhra Pradesh; in several places (like the village in this story), Hindus also participate in large numbers in the procession of relics during Peerla Panduga.

[2]**palakhova:** a traditional Andhra Telangana sweet made of condensed milk, sugar and ghee.

In Apoo's thoughts and dreams there is nothing and no one else other than Munnee.

It is so very surprising that she has neither spoken to nor played with Munnee these past five days! In that house, her father's tyrannical orders make even Apoo's maternal and her paternal grandmothers shiver. Then what about nine-year-old Apoo? Even so, she must go to see Munnee and return, even if by stealth! But Apoo is scared that just like in the thief and police game, she will get caught.

"Arey, don't you go even by mistake in the direction of Munnee's house. Your nanna has eyes at the back and the front! Don't know how he comes to know, but he comes to know...and your back will be soundly thrashed!" nanamma has already warned her. How can Apoo forget what happened one day when she had gone, and how her nanna had beaten her when she had returned.

"Why are you killing a flower-like child by thrashing her like this?" nanamma had intervened. But nanna does not care who is in front of him at such moments and he will just shove them aside with one hand! "Arey, Suresh, you are not even capable of distinguishing between the old and the young!" Saying this, nanamma had left angrily.

The day Apoo had brought home the horse doll, Suresh had shouted at her in rage, "If you dare step into that house again, I won't keep quiet," and he had gone away to the night bhajan at the temple.

That's it! From that day, all talk between Apoo and Munnee stopped. Their playing together stopped. It caused so much trouble that the crow from this street would not go and caw in that street.

But Apoo somehow saved her beloved horse doll from all that commotion by throwing it under the chair, and praying, "Jai Peer Baba, save Chamki from these blows!" No matter what kind of difficulty it is, if you think of Peer Baba, it disappears just like this. Isn't that what Fatammagaru said the other day? It seems Peer Baba came to their village on that very horse. A very long time ago when a great battle took place, after completely annihilating all the enemies, it seems that he got onto that same horse and rode away somewhere. That is why on the walls of the peerla chavidi there are so many pictures of horses. Those were the horses on which Peer Baba rode away to safety. All the people in the village believe that they are sacred horses.

At this moment it does not matter to Apoo whether it is a Rama or a Peer Baba, but someone who will listen to her woes and make Munnee and her meet! That's all!

"Satyamma! Here, I have brought something for you!" Saying this, a month ago their neighbour Aruna's mother gave Apoo's mother a calendar full of pictures of peers. It seems she bought it in a fair in the neighbouring village during the peer festival of that village. After praying to the peers in this village, Aruna's people would also go to the neighbouring village to attend the peer festival there. Aruna's mother said that the powers of that peer, who was killed very young in the battle, were even greater.

"If the picture of that peer is in the house, no evil powers will dare enter. Thinking that may niyyat and barkat, good intentions and prosperity always be with you, I brought this for you," said Aruna's mother.

"Akka, you know this, don't you—these days my husband does not like anything Muslim, Muslim pictures, Muslim words..." Satyamma was about to tell Aruna's mother. But would she listen!

"Everyone goes to the peer fair. This is our village custom. Aren't you and Ramesh's people the only ones who don't pay heed to the ways of the ooru and wada, the village and its poorer neighbourhood? Why, Satyamma? When I saw this calendar, I thought of you. Take it, Satyamma! Put it on the wall of your house. It will protect your home!" Saying this, Aruna's mother placed the calendar in Satyamma's hand, and left.

When she heard Ramesh's name, Satyamma felt the anger rise sharply within her. "That Ramesh, he comes here once a week and makes your nanna and three other temple elders sit down and talk all kinds of unnecessary things, like 'our dharma' and 'their dharma'.

'That is not our religion, that is not our dharma. Our dharma is Ganga water, and their dharma is a desert!' Such things we heard only from Ramesh for the first time."

On hearing that name, Apoo immediately asked her mother, and not once but twice, "Amma, what is dharma? What is religion? Are they some new kind of dolls?"

"Amma, isn't it because of that Ramesh uncle that we have stopped going to the peer festival? How wonderful it is to go to that festival! All my friends would meet there. We would play. Eat a lot. Don't our next-door neighbours, Aruna's people also go to the peer festival? It is our festival too, isn't it, amma? We can also go, can't we, amma?"

"You don't understand, Apoo...Nanna does not like it. That is not our custom. Isn't your nanna an elder to all the people in our village? As an elder doesn't he have to advise everyone? If he himself goes to Muslim fairs and to peer fairs, then our people in these four villages will get spoilt. In fact, these are not good times for us and for our people," Satyamma said. Perhaps she did not know what more to say, so she kept quiet.

"Nanna does not like it." Apoo understood up to that point. But what was said thereafter went above her head.

That day, not knowing what to do with that calendar, Satyamma hung it in a corner of the front room so that it was hardly visible.

But, it still caught Suresh's eye. That's it! A battle like the one between Rama and Ravana began to rage in the house. When it was over, what Apoo understood once more was that, unlike in Aruna's house, they could not have pictures of other gods and such in their house.

How Apoo adored the gods' room in Aruna's house! One Sunday when they were playing, Aruna took her into that room. So many pictures adorned the wall; not just pictures, on a small platform like a wedding mantap there were idols of Sita and Rama, Siva and Parvati, Vinayaka, along with photos of peers and peer temples...Aruna showed her all these. But what Apoo loved most above all was the calendar with the picture of the chamki-flowered horse! That shining, silky wool thread...the symbol of the hand on its flank! She had heard in the stories told by Aruna's mother and Munnee's mother that the name of that hand was the Hand of God.

While she was examining that picture keenly, Aruna took out sacred ash from a vessel and put it on Apoo's forehead. That was the ash brought from the peerla gundam, the fire pit of the peers. Aruna said that if one touched it to the eyes reverentially and put it on, all the pain in the heart would disappear.

Immediately rubbing it off, Apoo said, "Ammo, nanna will get angry."

Aruna's mother said, "Okay. Each to one's own custom. Nothing will happen. You sit here, I'll get you some snacks." She made Apoo sit in the front room, and brought her chakkilalu and ariselu. That's why Apoo adored Aruna's mother! How many different kinds of tasty dishes they would make, and for each festival! For that matter, every time Apoo came to their house, it was a feast for her!

"Attayya! Please tell me the story of this chamki-flowered god!"

"O, the peer god...?" said Aruna's mother, and she started telling her the story. When she heard the full story, Apoo fell in love with that peer god! As soon as Aruna's mother had finished narrating, Apoo announced, "Attayya, this peer god is my favourite!"

Little did naïve Apoo realise that this announcement of hers that day would go such a long way in distancing her from Munnee.

"If we constantly move with others, we will behave just like them! Did you listen to me when I told you not to send her to that wretched Muslim house!" nanna was admonishing amma again that morning.

Apoo was waiting to see what amma would say in response.

It was only much later that she began to understand that, for her nanna, all others were "others".

Nanamma had no such problem. She would pray to Rama and she would also pray to the peer. If one asked her anything more, she would say, why, both are the same, aren't they? Aruna's mother too would not touch anything before she did her pooja every day. Likewise she would also pray to the peer. Aruna would not step out of the house before she had bowed before the peer. Lakshmi's mother would not begin her day's work before going to the peerla chavidi every morning as soon she got up and touching its steps in reverence. So, did they all or didn't they all believe in god?

In Suresh's view, all those were wrong things. It seems these were not dharma! Only if one went to the temple it was dharma or it augured well. All the rest—that is, playing and singing the peer gods' songs, praying to them, going to the peerla chavidi just like they went to the temple, bringing back pictures of peers and keeping them at home—all these were wrong things. That meant that our people ought not to do any of these things!

When Munnee gave her the chamki-flowered horse doll, Apoo could not say no. She hid it in her frock and brought it home. She knew what would happen if her nanna were to see it. Moreover, it was very difficult to keep such things away from nanna's sight.

Apoo did not realise that the day she brought the doll home would be the last day that she would play with it.

She was mad with anger at her nanna and his beliefs for he said she could not go to Munnee's house and that she could not play with Munnee. Amma could at least find fault with him. Nanamma chatted with Apoo about all kinds of things, but she didn't dare ask her, "How come you are not playing with Munnee today?" For them, this was not such a big problem.

"Don't know in which world this fellow is living?" nanamma would grumble. "In this village, I can't remember thinking of 'us' and 'them' at any time," she had told amma once. No matter what nanna said, amma and nanamma kept going to the peer temple without nanna's knowledge. The others too, like Aruna's mother, would go to the temple, and they would also go to the peerla chavidi and pray to the pictures there!

But Apoo didn't want any of these. What did she want? She only wanted to play with Munnee for a while, sing with her, help her decorate her dolls, chat happily with those dolls together with

Munnee for a while. Only that much! But...just for this, to go so far...?

Thinking deeply about all of this, we don't know when Apoo has slid into sleep. In her sleep she is in her own world, running about in the peer procession with Munnee. The Saheb who is carrying the peer is finding it very difficult. But the minute both Munnee and Apoo shout, "Jai Anjaneya!" it is as if the Saheb gets a mountain of strength and is able to carry the peer easily.

The world in Apoo's sleep is full of excitement. In her sleep she utters only two words aloud—"Jai Peer Sami!" and "Munnee!"

These two words are heard by Satyamma who has just come in to cover Apoo with a sheet. Apoo is fast asleep. Between her hands is the chamki horse that she has hugged tightly to her chest.

Satyamma is about to take away the doll from Apoo's hands, but Apoo does not let her! Evading her hands, Apoo turns aside, hugs it even tighter and sleeps in a crouched position. While doing so, she again talks in her sleep: "Munnee, I'll come again tomorrow!"

Satyamma sits on the side of the cot and places a hand on Apoo's forehead—it feels warm.

Just then, Suresh steps into the house, calling out, "Amma!"

Though he has only called out to his mother, Satyamma answers softly out of habit, "Look...I am here with the child."

Suresh says, "Okay," from outside.

"Apoo seems a bit unwell. I am with her."

Satyamma is hopeful that at least then Suresh will come in and see Apoo. She wants to tell him in her own words all that is on Apoo's mind.

"Has she eaten?" he asks from the room outside.

"No she hasn't. She has not been eating well," Satyamma says as she herself comes out of the room.

Suresh sees that Satyamma is about to tell him something. But Suresh does not wish to speak much just then, partly because he does not want to disturb Apoo's sleep and partly because he is in a rush to go out.

Gulping down two morsels hurriedly and immediately getting up to leave, he says, "You know, don't you, that we have been going about collecting money for the temple. In this small village it is a humungous task to collect even a few rupees. At this time of the day, Ramesh and I have to go to two or three houses."

Unable to say anything more, as soon as he leaves, Satyamma comes in and sits near Apoo. She looks intently at Apoo's sleeping face. She remembers how she was at Apoo's age, how mischievously playful she was! It has been so long since she imagined herself that young! That innocence, that ability to mingle with others just like that! Nanamma says Apoo takes after Satyamma.

She keeps looking in amazement at the innocence, the childishness and the naiveté on Apoo's face.

Perhaps Satyamma has never looked at Apoo so closely before. On that innocent sleeping face all kinds of shadows flicker. Dark shadows. Shadows Satyamma had never seen or known in her own childhood. How times have changed! How much they have changed everything, especially her family. Her Apoo! Even as she watches, she wonders if her child is becoming lonely.

She tries to imagine the absolute joy on Apoo's face when she plays with Munnee.

She draws Apoo even closer.

"She's just a small child. What else would she know at her age? For her that god-doll is only a play-doll and nothing else. She will play with it for a while, that's it! What's the point in bringing god into children's games? What's the point in telling her about devotion, about dharma, things that she can't even understand?"

She must say these things to Suresh sometime. But will there ever be a time when she can open up her heart and speak to him freely? Perhaps not. Seeing the tail and muzzle of Apoo's chamki-flowered horse peeking out of the sleeping child's tight embrace, Satyamma smiles gently to herself. At that moment she feels, no matter what happens, she herself would go and drop Apoo at Munnee's house.

Suresh would never allow this. But can she go and drop her child? Does she, Satyamma, have that much courage? She has to see how far she can go! Satyamma is lost in thought.

Meanwhile, Apoo, who has been roaming the whole wide world with Munnee in her dreams, does not know this. Turning towards her mother, Apoo hugs her doll even closer...as if she is hugging Munnee!

Originally published in Telugu as 'Chamkipoola Gurram'
in *Aadivaram Andhra Jyothy*, 25 October 2015, pp. 64–73.

5. Behind a Door

"Arey, Faiz, come here once at least this month. I'm worried about Anwar. He may not be with us for too long...It is up to you then." Saying this Saheb mamu put down the phone.

Have to go...Must go...Must be with Anwar at least during these last few days. But will I really be able to? Will I be able to look into his sharp eyes? Will I be able to talk to his lifeless figure when all his thoughts have turned into a wasteland?

Moving my left hand in front of my eyes, I looked at my watch. Why did I look time and again into the fearful tiger-like face of this watch? I felt an inexplicable anxiety, almost a fear. As I looked at the two hands that appeared to have stopped, listened unwillingly to their silence...this room, this watch, these books, these paintings—I and this profound hidden, formless silence...

"It is criminal for you to remain completely silent! Speak up! Express everything—voice it, open your heart! Otherwise you have no being at all!" Anwar would say. Each time I recollected those words, I would feel like speaking out. But I remained like a well that had been closed for ever. A dry step well of the old times with not a drop of water. Would I ever be able to speak out directly and clearly like Anwar? Perhaps not.

In fact, all those that had given me courage were now causing me anxiety. On the wall, my favourite Dali painting, *The Persistence of Memory*. In that painting, a pocket watch melting away, a shape congealed in a trance, ants looking at the watch, listening, imagining, dreaming—though I was pulled into the same silence, repeating similar words and remaining there, my involvement with the outside world was shrinking. My lonely room. Books, some paintings, a bit of music...A world that had everything but people! In this job with a magazine, there is always the suspicion whether the person next to me is a human being or not! Fences all around words.

"Faiz, there's an escapist in you. Get rid of him quickly! Otherwise all your talent is just moonshine during the day!" Isn't that so? Is what is within me escapism? Was I even trying to escape that question?

When we were in the first year of Intermediate, Anwar did not just write slogans on the wall at midnight, he tried to find out the impact of those slogans on his life. Slowly, from teaching in a small school to feed his stomach, he went to the big political schools where the party leaders taught, studying again, learning. Did I understand what distances he traversed, and what he was searching for so intently? Perhaps not. As I moved on in life, becoming a coward with uncertainty as my path, he, amidst several obstacles, stood true to "his own self". All that was left for me was the dream that the two of us might meet sometime.

I lay down pulling the sheet over my body and up to my face on the same bed that had carried me many nights and some daytimes these past ten years. It was eight-thirty at night this Sunday. I would not get sleep at this time. In fact, I did not get sleep easily at any time. I had to buy sleep in the form of pills.

It was not winter. Not even rainy season. It was the peak of summer. Even though the fan was on, I was sweating. It seemed as if the harsh hot winds of the afternoon were continuing to blow through the windows.

Turning my head to a side, I looked towards the book shelf on the right. Whenever I looked at the books I would be distraught wondering where we had begun and where we had emerged. It would make me recall the journey I was unable to make along with Anwar even though I was with him. Was it mere recollection? I was totally bewildered. It disturbed the imaginary layers that I had covered myself with. Then, had Anwar entered me much more deeply than I had thought...? Don't know! There was nothing that

Anwar did not do to pull me out of the step well. I was so fond of escaping into my thoughts that I would not return to reality!

At such a moment, I received Saheb mamu's phone. Almost as if he had got the message that I was getting sucked into something. Mamu was calling out to me as if he wanted to pull me out of that bog. Today he also said another thing: "I know, Anwar is the only one for you!"

"Who is Anwar? What is Anwar?" There are no easy answers to questions like these.

To me, Anwar meant many things...thoughts, experiences, books...his motionless body on the sick cot. "Take all these books. I don't feel like reading anything!" The night Anwar said this was one of those long sleepless nights.

A few books that Anwar bought lovingly or swiped, the people he himself went in search of. My desire was to remain a clean slate, wiping away everyone and everything completely, without my being different from him, and without getting involved in any political issues. That desire would not be fulfilled. That was because I did not know my own form. That was because I myself did not know in what frame I could fit in.

One afternoon Sahana too left my room saying the same thing.

"You have to fit into some frame. It may not be necessary for everyone, but you at least need it. I too, who wants to share my life with you, need it."

Sahana did not leave in a rush. She did not leave in anger either. She left with love and compassion. She left with some belief that she would return some day like a lamp that had not been extinguished. Three years!? Did not know. Did not remember where my time stopped. Oblivion—I am one oblivion. Oblivion like Anwar. An oblivion that had frozen only in Sahana's memories even though she had left.

"What do you read? You are not absorbing what you read. You are living merely in words. You have to become a sentence. The beauty of the words is not allowing you to think." Anwar who said this had slipped into a state of thoughtlessness when the brain refused to work. But I was refusing thought even though I had a brain.

Not one memory that would let me be still. Stagnant water that would not let me move forward.

Lifeless on the cot—yes, wasn't it so, how well the poet Eliot said it—"Like a patient etherized upon a table". Perhaps when Katyayani Madam discussed that poem for the first time in class, I did not realise that it would haunt me all these years. Just on that poem I wrote a twenty-five page essay—don't know why I wrote it, but I did write it then! Though Madam said, laughing, "Just think, it might be a problem if you get so emotional! Neither life nor study is just an impression, nor is it just an emotional outburst. If you just stop at appreciating what Eliot says or what Engels says, it won't do. Beyond that appreciation and emotional outburst, what are you as a critic?" But the impressionistic language I used even now was just that. That hadn't changed even now.

"You have to change! If you don't change you are a burden to those around you! A bit of reason and practicality is necessary," Sahana had said this once. In those days, I too said a lot of things in jest. In that vein, I recited these few lines I borrowed from Eliot to Sahana—those words that I had recited then have now remained as a poster on my wall. This was another of those nights that I was reading them again:

> Time for you and time for me,
> And time yet for a hundred indecisions,
> And for a hundred visions and revisions,
> ...
> In a minute there is time
> For decisions and revisions...[1]

[1] T. S. Eliot, 'The Love Song of J. Alfred Prufrock'.

"Faiz, decide on something and then set out. If you delay any further, Anwar will remain only a guilty memory for you. Come... come and spend these last few days with him at least."

There was nothing in Saheb mamu's tone. No tears in his eyes perhaps. He would have practised hard to be able to speak like that, without tears, cutting off all emotions. To speak of emotions so logically, so rationally...must have been difficult!

But, would I be able to go to Anwar again? Perhaps not.

"Arey, Faiz, you're never ready for anything! That's just not possible for you. By the time you finally wake up in your eleventh hour, what was to happen would have happened! You'd be there only to say goodbye!"

Sahana said this laughing. Now there wasn't even much scope left in my mind to say goodbye. From where was Sahana able to get that wave after wave of laughter? In that little time together my world would be brightened majestically. But after her departure, darkness once again. Again I would lapse into a monologue. I was a clown who went behind the screen and cried my heart out! The tears I had forcefully controlled—a torrent, a flood!

By the way, would I be able to see Anwar?

I got up from bed and stood hiding my face in my hands. Anwar was standing tall in front of me, like a life-sized painting. Though, he was not an abstract painting like me—he was an abstract painting that was slightly readable! "Are you coming? Or you won't come?" he was saying, looking keenly into my eyes.

Perhaps Anwar was lucky that he was not Faiz. Would anyone know what hellish doors he was passing through, dragging himself? Even I who had the illusion of seeing myself as his reflection would not know perhaps!

For that matter, Anwar had always appeared to be like the outer form of my several inner battles. If one were to draw a single figure out of all the crooked and tangled lines within me, it would merge into a portrait called Anwar! That is why whenever I saw Anwar, whenever he came to mind, a slight trepidation, a little tremor, a great dilemma that could never be resolved.

Was this why I was not ready to face Anwar even now?

But in fact, it was always difficult for me to face Anwar.

For that matter, I was terrified of those who spoke about the next day. Not about political forecasts, but more importantly, about life; from the constantly changing situations around us now, to predict tomorrow in any manner worried me. Along with other things, Anwar had the great ability to talk about tomorrow. Whenever he spoke of tomorrow, he would speak so logically. One spoke of cause and effect, right? Anwar had, from the very beginning, the ability to unambiguously grasp that relationship.

Many things happened later...much, much later. During the nights that we roamed about the old city which was being crushed under curfew, the many sleepless nights that we spent talking about Gujarat that had in vengeance slaughtered and cast away even the blobs of blood growing in the womb. But...when was the first time that I saw the anger and the anguish in him? I had to keep excavating Anwar's story to touch my own silent depths.

At a time when we shared our childhood and youth in the same village, there would always be activities we liked, places we liked. For instance, Ramdas's tea stall adjacent to the big masjid in Common Bazaar was the favourite haunt of Anwar, Raghu, Jaffer, Leelaprasad and me. No matter where we were or where we might have gone, by the time it was six all five of us would gather there. Not just for tea but also for Ramdas's news. There would always be a sand heap against the masjid wall. Sitting on the heap we would chat for hours without count. A few truths, a few dreams, some teenage anxieties—everything! In all this, Ramdas was an experienced narrator.

I remembered clearly the summer evening we met the day the Intermediate final year exams were over, getting up happily after the afternoon nap, our faces pleasantly swollen.

That day Leelaprasad had brought his homemade special mysorepak and also khara. There were of course Ramdas's famous mirchi bhajjis. Just then Jaffer too had come from the masjid after reciting the Quran. Raghu had already informed us that he would be a little late that day, so we had not looked out for him. Anwar and I had thought of visiting the library from the tea stall itself, and had brought along two bags full of library books.

As soon as we had arrived, Ramdas had said, "Enough of studies, babu...the exams are over, right? Now go enjoy yourselves! Why books again?"

"Leave me aside, but this Anwar can't sleep without books." I was used to speaking in this familiar manner since childhood, as if I had authority over Anwar in such matters.

But it was indeed Anwar who read the most in that group. Having read all the course books in the summer break, he would be quite at ease during the rest of the academic year. Just browsing through text books, he would read all the books that he liked to read—Urdu poetry, Urdu stories, English poetry. He would cry hoarse that it was not possible to put your thoughts in the right direction unless you read. He kept a small note board on his wall on which he would note down the title of the book he had to read that week. That's it! That meant he would effortlessly read a book a week!

That did not however mean that books were Anwar's only world. "Books refine your thoughts only to a certain extent. How keenly you observe your surroundings is also important. If you find a rhythm between the two, then the experience of reading books becomes musical!" Anwar would say.

Diametrically his opposite, I would read poetry or literature only for its aesthetic beauty—then, and even now. It is in fact only Anwar who made me think and see differently, in so many ways. It is his thoughts that have in part laid the foundation for my search for a life as a journalist. But the sheer beauty of language would not make me move or budge.

That day we had played doodumpulla[2] in the sand. It was actually a game little children played, but that evening we had wanted something different. That too unplanned. After having played for a while, as if he had suddenly remembered that he was

---

[2]**doodumpulla:** a children's game where a thin stick is hidden in the sand to be discovered by the opponent.

seventeen, Anwar had said, "Abbey, we can play such games only for a while. We can remain like children only for a while. We cannot be so after that. That's the irony of age!" Saying this, he had turned towards the masjid wall. And that was it, he had suddenly slid into silence.

After a while, the other three had left, giving us high-fives and saying, "We'll make a move now, ra! Phir milenge! Will meet again tomorrow."

Like always, Anwar and I had stayed back. Because we used to live in the same locality.

I had looked into Anwar's face—it was bereft of the earlier excitement. In that dusky darkness, in that dim light from the distant street lamp, Anwar's face had been clearly visible. On that face, I saw uncountable shadows. A little fear, some irritation too—that was the first time I saw his face reflecting those mixed emotions.

"Okay, get up now, I am famished," I had said, getting up from the sand heap. He too had got up.

We would have to walk at least half an hour to reach home from the big masjid.

I had looked into his face. There was no change. Anwar could never be silent like this when we were walking together. He would pick up some topic and start speaking. He would talk, thinking for a long time between words, as if he was peeling each layer by layer, asking me for responses in-between, egging me on, pushing out sentences from within me.

But that day it had seemed as if he would not open his mouth. If he did not open his mouth, I would not be able to sleep that night, trying to find meanings to his silence.

I had kept waiting. Finally, I had to ask.

"What's the matter?"

"Didn't you see it then? Come let's turn back and go to the big masjid." Saying this, he had taken me back, almost dragging me along with him.

By the time we reached there, Ramdas had almost closed his shop. Except for one or two people, there had been no one on the road. As soon as we had reached, placing his index finger on the masjid wall, Anwar had said, "Look...Read...Don't you see anything? Really?"

I had kept reading, "Musalmanon ke do hee stan—Pakistan ya kabristan. Only two places for Muslims—Pakistan or the graveyard."

"Did you ever hear this in our village before?"

"No!"

After that I had begun to notice the change that was coming over Anwar day by day. In tune with the insecurity that had been growing in our village, I could see the resulting changes on his face. In the ensuing changes, there was impatience, there was frenzy. There was a desire to do something. Slowly, he had turned into a silent revolution.

Before I could observe that change unfold completely, I got a job in a small magazine and went away to Vijayawada. My life then took a speedy road, and slowly, Anwar's world started to recede. In other words, it was I who distanced myself from the others and from everything. I was so entrenched in my silent bog that I did not go back to my village—until Saheb mamu called me up after the demolition of Babri Masjid. Following a heated exchange of words, the other party had beaten up Anwar badly. After that, Anwar did not remain Anwar.

I did go to see him then, but I did not stay with him for very long. I could not bear to see the Anwar I knew so bereft of words, thoughts and emotions. An infant who had lost everything, the naiveté of childhood that he had rejected all his life—I was unable to see that childlike quality in him. I kept remembering what he had said when we were in college.

"Abbey, we can play such games only for a while. We can remain like children only for a while. We cannot be so after that." As Anwar had said, was it irony related only to age? Seeing him now, I could not remain there watching how this world, how this whole world had cruelly played with him. On returning, I had immediately crept back into my burrow, burying myself in the sports page of the magazine.

After Anwar was gravely wounded, I lapsed into an even greater silence. So much so that my being was not conscious that I "existed"! There was only one difference—no one had attacked me, no one was going to kill me. No one was going to kill Anwar either. True. I was able to understand then how one is not killed at one go but served death piecemeal every moment.

> How should one talk about death now?
> Who will listen? To the moans of my inner wounds?
> In this weak body not a drop of blood remains
> The last but half a drop is not a light
> Not even a hint of moisture
> It cannot douse the fire, nor can it quench the thirst!

I could hear the voice and the words of the great poet Faiz resounding within me.

I could never understand why father named me Faiz. But I now realised that Faiz wrote these lines just for me. Now when I was nothing…for that matter, when I was always nothing!

"Anwar is no more. You did not come. I had thought that you wouldn't come. But the last look, the deedaar, is the final gift that we can give to the one we love. You did not give him even that, Faiz. You did not give him anything!" Saying this, Saheb mamu had put down the phone when he had called after two or three days.

I cannot now remember whether it was two days or three.

Originally published in Telugu as 'Oka Talupu Venaka' in *Andhra Jyothy*, 21 August 2016; in *Kooradu-2013, Telangana Kathala Sankalanam*; and in *Sahil Vastadu: Mari Konni Kathalu* by Afsar (Hyderabad: Chaya, 2019), pp. 74–83.

6. Saheli

"It is wonderful that they have named you Shabnam."

I could not ignore these words of Arjun, walking two or three feet behind me. Should I turn back or not? How could I face the one who had uttered these words? Should I slap him with words or hit him with a chappal? Or, should I perhaps conceal these words beautifully in the inner recesses of my heart without doing anything? I felt I must turn around once and, if possible, look into his eyes. Wonder what emotion was visible in those eyes when he was speaking those words.

In fact, those words did not appear so cheap at that moment.

Without turning back to look, I kept walking briskly. Just this year left to complete the degree—that was all I wanted! Saying this to myself, on ammee's insistence I would read the Ayatul Kursi protection prayer every day—not once but ten times—remembering the thousand names of Allah and doing mannat at Maulali Darga, praying for a boon.

Hope this stupid body won't come in the way of my getting the degree! Whenever ammee heard me say such things, she would promptly sing the tune, "Stop these stupid studies!"

When I neared the college, I turned around once to look. Arjun was not there! Had he gone away? Really?

It wasn't long since I heard those words…had he really vanished in just five minutes? I couldn't believe it. As soon as I entered college, near the steps to the classroom, Janimiyan, the attendant, saw me and said, "Kya hai, Shabnam beti? Why study anymore? Just have a nikkah happily…But perhaps your abbajaan will not perform a nikkah but do a registered marriage!" He did not seem to be mocking me. His smile showing his red paan-stained teeth seemed pleasant. Janimiyan would always say this! But this time, his words were a bit…for some reason it just seemed to me that he said this because he had overheard Arjun.

Was nikkah the only thing left for me now? Did I have to have a nikkah? Registered marriage? Love first? Marriage first? Ammee would say love after marriage. Abbajaan would say it was love that mattered most. "Don't teach her all the useless things of your English studies!" ammee would say angrily. If only I had the choice and a voice in the matter of marriage, in the matter of such a relationship! Was that even possible?

If only I could just turn around once and take a quick look! Yes…I saw.

A little distance away, behind that tree, Arjun…waving his hand! Even at this distance, Arjun's smile appeared beautiful. Was his smile really beautiful? Or, did it just seem like that to me at this moment?

I could not say. I could not say anything.

Ohho…Did I have dreams of love and marriage then? Even if I had such imagination or dreams, they would have vanished after Haseena aapa's marriage, and later, her talaq. Though abbajaan did not have much faith in Islamic traditions, unable to say no to ammee, how traditionally and how splendidly he had performed her nikkah! With whatever little money he had, how grandly was the wedding organised! It also collapsed in such a terrible fashion. After two years, Haseena aapa had returned home. After another fortnight, Haseena aapa left home and went away. Till today we don't know where she went or what happened to her.

Having seen Haseena aapa's husband Rehman, I had felt disgusted with men. "That was a big mistake in my life. I should never have got her married into such a traditional family!" abbajaan would always say with regret. In fact, I could never understand why he did! "But why did you agree?" When I had asked her this, Haseena aapa had said, "At that time, he had seemed good enough to me. Considering all the Muslim youngsters of today, I had felt Rehman was okay the way he was."

"Why only a Muslim youngster? Did you want him to be like Ameer or Meer in Chalam's novels?"

"At that time, amidst all these Hindu-Muslim problems, I thought a fellow Muslim was better. No matter how progressive a Hindu is, I could have no faith in him. Among Muslim youth, 'progressive' has almost become a dirty word. What was the way out? When ammee-abba insisted that I get married, I thought let the marriage be performed according to their wishes...I thought I could get adjusted later."

"You really had no clarity then, aapa? You took marriage so lightly! Actually, you need not have got married at all, right?"

If Haseena aapa's marriage and talaq was one story, there was another story that no one knew about—a story that I had kept entirely to myself, and not told abbajaan or ammee or anyone else. When they had been newly married, Rehman had asked me to make tea for him when no one was around, and as I was making tea, he had come and hugged me tightly from behind. I had turned around and hurled the tea vessel at him. It had missed the target and fallen elsewhere. But if it had actually fallen on his face, that story would have been known to everyone that day itself.

That was the first male touch in my life. I did not know that the male touch was such a disgusting experience. I wondered if, after giving that touch a name—that of a lover or a husband—that experience would change. Even if one were to give it such a name, remembering brother-in-law encircling me like a snake from behind, I would often feel that it would be better not to have to experience that touch at all.

Today, Arjun's smile and listening to his words from a distance made me feel good. Was my body ready to accept the experience of Arjun's touch if he were to come near me and touch me? Perhaps. Perhaps not—I could not tell.

That evening, when Baby came home—her real name was Harika—I was immersed in those thoughts. That evening she looked all the more beautiful in a light blue onee, a half-saree.

Baby had a lovely complexion. The light blue colour enhanced her beauty. If I saw someone in an onee like that, my eyes would turn green with envy! When I said that I would also wear an onee, ammee at once said a categorical no.

"No. Onee is not our custom. The whole body is visible in it. Should so much of the body be visible?" she said angrily.

As soon as Baby came, ammee said, "I'll go give this kheer to Sujatamma and come. You sit for a while." She packed a box, and left wearing a burkha—ammee would not step outside without a burkha. I would be very surprised when I thought how abbajaan's leftist ideology had not influenced ammee even a bit. When she would get irritated seeing all the books by Marx and Chalam on the desk, and say, "What's this? Why these bearded faces in the house all the time?" abbajaan would burst out laughing and say, "Aren't bearded Muslim men alone the ones that you like?"

Other than that, abbajaan would not discuss any matter at length with ammee. Even with us he would not begin a discussion unless we asked him something specific. "You must like it, be interested in it on your own first. After that, a discussion or anything else!" he would say. "I am not a preacher. Even in class I do not preach. I don't think that's my trait," he would say. As for me, I would think that abbajaan ought to tell us things, discuss things.

As I was immersed in my thoughts, I did not realise that I was in fact looking intently at Baby's blue onee without blinking. "What looks, babu! Will you eat me up? If you want to, then why don't you try it on?" said Baby.

Aha! This was the right opportunity! I took Baby inside the house.

"Baby, give me the onee…please!" I pleaded with her.

She took it off and gave it to me. I wore that blue onee and stood in front of the mirror.

"Its beauty won't be visible on top of a pyjama! Here, wear this also." Saying this she was about to take off the lehenga as well.

"Oh no, no...ammee will come back!"

"It doesn't matter." And tying a towel around herself, Baby gave me all three—the lehenga, the blouse and the onee. "But here, you must put them on right here!"

"Ammo! I feel shy!"

"It doesn't matter. I am not Arjun, right?"

"Aa...Arjun?"

"Yes...don't I know? Okay, now put them on."

I wore that blue onee in a second and stood before the mirror.

Standing in front of me, Baby said, "Aha! Now if only you would wear an onee and go out, not just Arjun, all the youngsters in town will be blown off their feet! Any colour will suit your physique very well. In this blue you look perfectly ravishing!" And then she was all over me and started kissing me. Before I even realised what was happening, she had pushed me onto the bed and started caressing me all over my body, softly murmuring, "Shabna, Shabna..." I do not recollect for how long.

After a little while, I got scared and I firmly pushed her away. She was about to hold my hands like a guilty person.

"Go away...Don't touch me!" I pulled off the onee quickly and threw it on her face.

"Don't say that...As soon as I touched your hand, something happened to me. I've made a mistake." Saying this, Baby wore the onee and ran out.

I found I was sweating profusely as I wore my shalwar kameez and stood in front of the mirror.

Ammee came in just then.

"Why in front of the mirror at this time? Come into the kitchen...there are a lot of dishes!" Saying this, ammee went into the kitchen in a huff.

Finishing all the tasks quickly, I got onto the bed and decided to pretend I was sleeping.

I felt as if a cool breeze was wafting by, touching my body delicately. At all the places Baby had touched, there were sweet tremors in my body. How would it feel to walk amidst five or six jasmine vines on a cool evening? Wouldn't one feel as if the fingers of that fragrance were caressing the body here and there? In those caresses, for a few moments I felt Baby's fingers, for a few moments Arjun's fingers...within me, a strange scene. But I was unable to cut off this scene quickly. Just like a circle spreads into many circles when a stone is thrown into water, that scene was spreading itself within me in all kinds of ways.

First what did Baby do? Then where did she touch me? I was placing that entire scene that lasted only a few minutes into a new frame, and viewing myself again and again within that frame, I slid into sleep at some late hour.

But, I slipped away from my own hands without knowing it after just those few minutes of experience! I began to realise that from now on I would involuntarily look out on some evenings for Baby. Before I went to sleep that night, there wasn't even an inkling in my mind that next morning my life was going to take a turn.

That turn: Arjun opening his heart out.

I did not imagine that that morning, Arjun would meet me at the main entrance of the college. When as usual, Baby and I were enjoying ourselves, cracking jokes and laughing, Arjun came up from behind us and stopped me, saying, "Shabnam, a word." Baby threw me a naughty smile, and walked a couple of steps ahead.

"I can't stop myself from telling you. I can't but love you. Can't forget you. I don't know what love is. I feel it is this, just this," he said in measured tones.

I looked into Arjun's eyes. His eyes were indeed calm. Steady smiling eyes. Eyes filled with love. Though I could not say immediately that that was love, I liked the confidence and steadfastness in those looks. Those eyes did not have the lust I had observed in the eyes of many youngsters. There was no compelling desire to eat you up. Those looks...yes, they reminded me of the blueness that I had borrowed on my body that day with Baby's onee. Actually, I didn't have the words now to express that emotion. I could not say. I could not say anything.

"I can't say. Can't say anything." Saying this I reached Baby in one leap.

Looking into my eyes, Baby said, "I understand," flying a naughty kite in her eyes.

Somehow, even that kite appeared blue to me, making me remember Baby's touch.

More than that, the naughtiness in Baby's eyes said something sweet to me that was stronger than Arjun's looks!

Till that evening, I felt suffocated. That evening, as it was turning dark and sliding slowly into moonlight, like a fistful of jasmines from my lap that were flowing into a thread and turning into a garland, I thought, "It'll be good if Baby comes!"

"Aapa, when Rehman touched you for the first time, what did you feel?" I had asked Haseena aapa a year after her wedding.

"What did I feel? Difficult to say. But it felt new. After the first night, I felt for the first time that I too had a body, that it had a world of its own, and that it spoke a different language."

"Really? You are reciting shayiri! Is that touch really like a poem?"

"It's difficult to say. You have to experience it for yourself and know it. Even if someone else were to explain you can't understand it." Saying this, aapa left, feeling really shy.

The second year too I had asked her the same question in a different way. I was unable to remember now how I had asked her. But aapa's response this time appeared strange to me.

"A man who cannot express desire is worse than an insect. When one forgets the joy in expressing desire, only sex remains between the two. Just a mechanical act. An act that kills the beautiful emotion. That's all."

"That means...?"

"That means...you won't know this too unless you experience it."

"How's that possible? This isn't like a job, is it? To go to another place if the experience here is not good! If this experience becomes strained, the bond itself will break, won't it?"

"Then...ammee and abba?"

Aapa had looked into my eyes as if to ask why I had brought up their topic.

"Yes, I know many things that you do not know. Before you could come to know some things, you became a part of another house, right? I have seen abbajaan repeatedly beating ammee hard on her back at midnight at least once a week and then going out and walking up and down, smoking one cigarette after another."

"I am unable to believe this. But these are not the times of ammee and abba. Now we know better than them what we want. We know what our hearts want. We know what our bodies want. Now we have some ideas about whose hands our bodies should fall into. Not that they did not have ideas. But having them is one thing, recognising that we have them is another. When you have the capacity to recognise what you want, then the mode of expressing desire changes."

"Is desire so powerful?"

"Certainly. It depends on the heat and intensity of the moment when desire takes over. At first, I saw that intensity in Rehman's touch. After that I did not have the strength to tolerate that brutishness in his intensity. If he were a wave of fire, I became a river that flows slowly. Then there was a difference of speed in our desires. The distance between the two speeds grew, and after that his speed turned into brutality. Then that desire lost its natural beauty."

"Ammo! Is there such a big story behind all this?"

"This is not a story, Shabnam. It is in fact the power that makes the bond between the two work! Without realising this, we search for insignificant reasons and we struggle."

"Aapa, you know I always thought that you would love and marry an Arvind, a Venkat or some other Hindu fellow. Finally, unable to say no to ammee, you fell in Rehman's path!"

"Yes, that was indeed a mistake! This time, I will not make a mistake," she had said smiling.

"This time means…that means…you will marry again?"

I could not believe that aapa had learnt so many things in just three years of marital life! But that was what I liked in aapa! She, unlike many others, did not wish to conceal the real thing and cover it with illusory layers. "Listen to what your experience tells you. It will never lie," aapa would say.

That is why, three months after she had left Rehman and come back home, she went away somewhere. There were rumours that she had eloped with someone. But before she had disappeared like that, she had talked to me for at least three hours.

"We are women. We look down upon our own experiences. We listen to all that men say for their own convenience. In our religion, men make us say that this is what is said in Islam. They will make us believe that we cannot behave in any other manner. That's why marriage is a big frame for us. If the woman lives constricted within that frame, then she is a good woman, otherwise, she is not a woman. That's the big lesson that living with Rehman taught me—that I can't be a woman like that!"

"Then, what kind of a woman are you?"

"I don't know yet. I can tell you what kind I am not. But I can't tell you what kind of woman I am so easily either."

"Will you get married again? Or…live together?"

"One thing is very, very clear to me. The frame of marriage doesn't seem to fit the womanliness in me. I can tell you just one thing—just because a marriage has failed does not mean you have failed. No matter where or how your marriage turns, you have to be yourself. This is in fact very difficult, but you have to remind yourself every moment that there is nothing more important than your own life. Marriage is just one chapter. You must be able to tear off a failed marriage as easily as you tear off a useless page in your notebook."

"How are you able to say this so firmly, so bluntly, aapa?"

"Once you are able to say it, you will know how to say it bluntly. More importantly for a woman, once you experience a touch filled with desire, depending on the way it changes you, your eyes will begin to open. That's the great education for a woman."

That night I had slept with a lot of thoughts!

After that, I had seen aapa only for three days and three nights. I had not seen her on the fourth night. Only questions remained within me. Not because of aapa's words, but for some reason, I began to have a kind of aversion towards a body that was male.

Yes, after that the body was a big question! I did not know that after a few days, a light would glow, and that that light would turn into Baby's body.

Arjun was at the main entrance of the college.

The two of us cultivated the habit of going together to the canteen to have tea. Sometimes Baby too would accompany us. But when Baby was around, I somehow found it awkward to talk to Arjun.

"Shabna, what have you thought about our future?" Arjun asked me one afternoon, dipping an Osmania biscuit in his tea.

"I haven't thought about it, really. We come here every day, have tea, that's all!" I was almost about to utter these words. But looking at Arjun's innocent face, I stopped. I didn't want to break his heart into pieces just then. I wanted to wait for some more time and reveal the reluctance in my mind.

But, what was my reluctance about?

"You mean...objection because you are a Muslim, and I a Brahmin?"

"Objection to what?"

"To love...to marry...?"

"I did not know that these two were now on our agenda, Arjun?"

"Why...? Didn't I tell you?"

"But, did I tell you anything?"

"No."

"Then...if the love is only on your part, it is not enough, right?"

"I somehow thought that you too had love for me."

"What can I do if you think in that manner? Only when I too feel something for you, it would mean mutual love, right?"

Arjun slipped into silence. As Baby walked in just then, a curtain fell on that ritual of silence.

"What, Arjuna, Phalguna!" Baby said playfully as she came in.

"What about Arjuna, Phalguna? Why just rain? He's caught in a big typhoon!" I said, laughing.

I don't know how I could say that at that moment! I seemed to have no control at all over my tongue, I thought. I looked at Arjun. The only thing he didn't do was cry! Patting him on his back and cajoling him somehow by saying, "Arey...I said it in jest! Come, let's go. We'll talk later," we took him along and went towards the classroom.

After that, I did not see Arjun for a week. I was a little worried. If I were to tell him, maybe his heart would be a little relieved...I wondered a couple of times if I ought to go to his house and tell him. Otherwise, would it be okay to tell him through Baby?

But something constrained my mind.

In the meanwhile, I had to go to Baby's house two or three times for some work. No, I purposely found some ruse to go there. As Baby's people were well to do, it was good that she had a room of her own upstairs. After that, I always found an excuse to go to Baby's house at least twice a week.

Our exams were due in a month.

Abbajaan had the opportunity to go to Libya the following year to teach English. He left for Libya a month ago. At home, just ammee and I...all alone!

When abbajaan was around, there was excitement, conversation, jokes. Abbajaan meant freedom, ammee meant restrictions. A great distance between the two. But what was I between these two powerful forces? This question used to perplex me no end. "At least on Sundays, sit calmly and finish reading the Quran at least, you demoness! You read all kinds of books...Can't you read just that one book?" Ammee's anger.

Sometimes the days would rush by as fast as seconds. Sometimes they seemed to give lame excuses as if to say they had to go very slowly.

Arjun was going about his studies in a routine manner. He had come out of the intoxication of my love much quicker than I had expected. That clear-headedness was what I liked about him! Sometimes he would come along with the two of us to have tea. In another six months' time, our degrees would be in our hands. There was always the question of what after that.

One day when I returned from college, I found a handsome youngster sitting at home. Ammee was speaking to him. As soon as I entered, ammee stopped speaking and introduced him to me.

"Saif. Do you remember? In the town, their family was close to ours. After that they shifted to Hyderabad."

Saif shifted slightly in an attempt to turn fully towards me. But it seemed as if he was very shy. That word shyness had never existed in my dictionary. That was why I sat looking directly at Saif. But his shyness was not put on. He was in fact feeling genuinely shy. Saif was really handsome. Good complexion. Pleasant face, clothes that reflected good taste. He left after talking for a while. There was nothing great in what he said. He did not seem to remember much about our town.

After he left, ammee said, "Saif is good-looking, right? Also has a good job. A computer job it seems. These days it's rare to find such boys among our people." I realised what ammee was about to say. She had been waiting impatiently for my degree to get over.

"Why the hell did this fellow have to come now?"

"What's that? Why are you saying such things? Why are you throwing out boys the way you throw out insects!"

"Ammee, he is really handsome. His salary too is beautiful. But I don't know if marriage has been written in my horoscope or not. That's what it is!" I said laughing. Though I had said those words laughing, I knew such words would explode a small bomb in ammee's heart. "This summer itself, I'll get someone or the other to tie the knot with you! I won't sit waiting for your response!" She too said this laughing and went into the kitchen.

That evening Baby came home. "Aunty, today we'll go to my house and study together." She started pleading with ammee.

"As if you listen to anything I say! Why plead at all? But not till late at night. Shabna, study for an hour or two and come back."

On hearing these words, Baby came close to me, pinched my waist, and said, "Hey, Shabbu, a surprise for you today."

"When have you not given me surprises?" Saying this, I followed Baby like a puppy that evening.

As soon as we went into the room upstairs, Baby said, "Shall I order food?"

"No...let's eat whatever is there at home."

"'Whatever is there' is not my philosophy. You like noodles and chicken pasta, don't you? It won't take long. Come, let's go to the kitchen." Saying this, she almost pushed me towards the kitchen.

"What...isn't aunty home?" I knew that Baby's mother would not be home on many evenings. But there was a relief in asking her that, and in Baby confirming, "No, mother isn't at home."

"Oho! Then the kitchen is our kingdom, right?" I said.

"Not just the kitchen..." Saying this Baby hugged me as I stood leaning against the edge of the table and kissed me, almost biting off my cheek.

"Sometimes you behave more atrociously than a man!"

"Oho, as if you have a lot of experience with men...!" Baby said, kissing me hard one more time.

Baby cooked and got everything ready in no time.

As soon as we went upstairs after eating, I said, "Abba, you served quite a lot of food! Now sleep is overpowering me!"

"Aha...will I let you off so easily?" Saying this, she opened a packet on the desk. She took out a dark blue onee, lehenga and blouse from it. She pulled me along to the dressing table.

"This colour looks gorgeous!" I said, and happily kissed Baby's cheeks to my heart's content.

"That's why I bought it! Go...try them on," she said. I was about to enter the bathroom.

"No...you must undress right here. Wear them right here too," ordered Baby.

Earlier, I would have felt very shy to do that. But now, I had lost that shyness. Even as Baby was looking, I removed my shalwar kameez and wore the dress she had bought right in front of her. Oh, the happiness in Baby's eyes!

Baby lay down on the bed and pulled me close to her. Her embrace provided me such comfort I felt I would nestle closer and closer in her arms and melt right away.

"Do you know ammee is very persistent about my marriage?"

"Is that true? With me, right?" She said this very coyly; then controlling herself, said, "What did you say?"

"Do I ever have the opportunity to say anything? Can I really tell ammee what I am thinking right now…what I could not even tell Arjun finally?"

"Then how long can you stop ammee?"

"I don't know…I haven't even started thinking about it in fact. I am also doubtful if I can tell abbajaan…"

"I know. I too can't reveal. But the question is whether one should expressly state it or not!"

"It may be possible for you not to say it. Not for me. We are middle-class after all, aren't we?"

"Yes, that may be so…" Saying this, Baby pulled me closer. Setting right the tresses on my forehead, pulling me close, she embraced me tightly. A wave of warm breath drowned me.

That was all I wanted for now!

But how long would this experience remain pure? Remain free?

I could not say…could not say anything.

It grew dark. Neither of us wanted to switch on the light in the room.

That darkness was sweet. Comforting.

A darkness that had no doubts at this point. A darkness that had no questions at this point. For this moment, a stable, serene darkness.

A darkness that was weaving a light between the two of us.

Originally published in Telugu as 'Saheli'
in *Sahil Vastadu: Mari Konni Kathalu*
by Afsar (Hyderabad: Chaya, 2019), pp. 84–99.

7. The Forest

The forest…A fat man. He has thrown him under his feet and is stamping all over him. Another man is dragging him and throwing him somewhere…

Someone somewhere is groaning…Someone else is carrying a girl's corpse…

He wakes up startled, gasping.

Darkness all around. He rubs his eyes and looks up. Can't see a thing. He gets up in fear and walks up and down. There is a stench. A youngster sleeps soundly nearby.

He rubs his eyes again. He feels as if all this has really happened. "Amma, amma…is not bedridden. Sister is not dead." He says this aloud to reassure himself, and lies down again, but…

He is unable to sleep. He wants to…but sleep eludes him. Time and again those shadows approach and stand before him. "Don't know if sister's wound has healed. Don't know how worried mother is! Does father even care at all? What grievous wrongs have I committed?"

No matter how much he tries, he is unable to sleep. Whether he closes his eyes or opens them, those shadows constantly move in front of him. That shop, the owner, that stupid youngster—everything appears like hell to him. It is as if he is caught in the jaws of some wild animal…as if his hands and feet are being cut off of their own accord. The looks of the owner as he is beating him—scalding looks that pierce the heart…The youngster's obvious pleasure on seeing him squirm…He doesn't know why he has to put up with all this for the paltry four and a half rupees he gets. His body is being crushed under the beatings he receives. There is nothing to do except to sit alone in a corner and mope. He keeps sobbing even in his sleep. He feels like crying out loud and collapsing. All his nights are drenched in tears. Red streaks fill his tired sleepless eyes.

"Young fellow...Will he be able to put up with it?" says mother.

God knows when ants got into his gunny sack. They start biting him. The youngster is still sleeping. An unbearable stench all around. Annoyed, he comes out and stands on the road.

Dawn is just breaking.

Rangadu sits in front of the shop and watches the passers-by. "Why are you sitting here?" Saying this, the owner enters. Thick moustaches, a protruding belly—he looks terrifying. Rangadu gets up slowly and follows the owner into the shop. They buy old newspapers and iron scrap.

Now the owner wakes up the stupid youngster who has covered himself with a sheet, and he goes out again. Not knowing what to do, Rangadu places stones on both the scales on the big balance and starts weighing them. The youngster rushes and gives Rangadu a whack on his back. When Rangadu asks him why, he gives him another. Rangadu sits crying. The youngster looks cruelly at him for a while and goes out.

"You and your woebegone face first thing in the morning!" Saying this, the owner wallops him as soon as he returns. The owner sits on a chair in front of a small table and pores into the account book.

In great fear and ever so slowly, Rangadu goes, picks up a small broom lying in a corner and starts sweeping the shop absentmindedly. The entire floor becomes blurred. His eyes start clouding with tears. He feels as if something is gnawing his brain.

When he got up in the morning, rubbed his eyes and looked out, it was already quite late. By then, mother had called out to him a couple of times and left it at that. If he did not get up even then, she would have to use force. It was not something he could forget so easily. Her beating would bring him to his senses no matter how deeply asleep he was. "You don't get up even when it is broad daylight. You are not human. Can't you listen if I tell you once?" Mother said as she combed out his sister's hair and killed the lice. His sister was swishing a piece of cloth in her hand, looking at it very closely and mumbling to herself.

Such a crazy girl! She would rummage through trash and collect all kinds of things. She would hide them somewhere and feel elated looking at them. She would converse with stones and trees and such, and while away her time. She would get up early in the morning, survey her vast empire and return.

He wanted to sleep again. He sat there swaying drowsily. He pulled the gunny sack that would habitually keep sliding away and was about to slowly go back to sleep. He was jolted awake when he saw the stick with cloth waist-threads[1] hung from it leaning against the tree. It had happened like this the previous day too. He had to receive blows from his father for having got up late. Without another squeak, he got up and washed his face. Wiping his face with his shirt, he cautiously looked to his right. His father was still snoring. No sign of his getting up soon.

Three days had passed by since they had come to this place. No sooner had they got off from the cart than they found this place. The village was not too far away. Though it was fruit-bearing season, that tree was shorn of leaves. As it was scorching hot, mother brought gunny sacks and old paper from somewhere and put up a roof. Even so it was difficult to tolerate the heat. But there was no other way out. Even if the father and son worked tirelessly and sold the waist-threads, they would not earn enough to feed themselves. Mother became jobless. How could someone give work to a person who lives one day here and the next day elsewhere? His sister was young, not even five or six.

Rangadu stood looking at the vessel on the stove. His eyes were burning. His belly was drawn in and looked pathetic. Wonder if

---

[1] **waist-thread:** black or red thread worn around the waist, with or without an amulet, to ward off evil; it is a custom common to several Hindu and Muslim communities in India.

there was any saddi[2] in the vessel or not! Since they came here, they had to set out without eating anything. Business was not good. What they got was not sufficient at all. Though they had stayed here for a week or a week and a half, they had not got enough to feed themselves. This was something they had never experienced before.

His looks shifted from the vessel to his mother. She continued to kill the lice on his sister's scalp. He hoped he would get an answer from his sister. Not a word from her, no matter how long he waited. Then he himself asked. Mother said there was no food, slowly shaking her head. He got angry with her that she said it so firmly. He felt knives churning in his stomach. Spitting fire, he picked up the vessel on the stove and flung it. It flew and fell far away on the stones there.

Pushing the girl aside, mother got up to bring back the vessel, and said raising her voice, "Is your stomach full now? Has it cooled down? No money…and you don't even have the sense to adjust. Haven't there been days when I have begged and brought food home? If I have any, won't I give…?!" She kept the vessel back on the stove.

"No. I won't go out even if I have to die." Saying this, he sat down adamantly.

"Father will get up!" she shouted.

"Let him get up." He was sullen.

"Both of you go to hell!" Saying this, she went back and put her fingers into the little girl's hair. He got wild with rage at this and started hurling things around. "Wretched bitch! Before I get up she licks every vessel clean!" Saying this, he picked up a stone and hurled it at his sister. She raised a hue and cry. She was hurt. It started bleeding.

"Wretch! What has befallen you!" mother screamed, pressing her paita to the girl's bleeding forehead. "What if it had hit her eyes? As it is, we don't live even a hand-to-mouth existence. How

---

[2]**saddi** or **saddannam:** leftovers of the previous night's rice soaked in buttermilk and fermented to be eaten as breakfast the next morning.

would you have fed her?" she said, and she started wailing. With this, there was no holding back the little girl's tears.

Father woke up irritated amidst all this commotion. "Demons! Won't let me sleep! What happened?" He shouted as if all hell had broken loose.

"What do you mean what happened? Look at your son's great deed!" Saying this, mother showed him the girl's forehead. Taking advantage of this, sister cried even louder.

Rangadu started trembling. He was terrified. If father got up, he would skin him alive. He looked this way and that, mustered all the energy at his command, and in the midst of his mother's screams and his sister's wails, he took to his heels.

Running, he came to the village. He ran on every road he found. Finally, gasping for breath, he came to the railway station and sat down on the bench inside. Perhaps a train was coming. The platform was crowded. Passengers were impatiently moving to and fro. Everything looked chaotic. The brain felt like a thick forest. He wondered why he had hit her. But why not, he thought! He had to roam about so much all day that his feet and knees would break. Did she not have the brains to think that she ought to leave something for him? He tried to reason in this way for a while. But this reasoning did not pacify him.

He could not sit there for very long. On these streets, there was no way that his father could spot him, he thought. He walked heavily, swinging his arms angrily. As he walked he felt annoyed with the road. Streets jam packed with people, rickshaws, cars. So much noise and commotion it would break one's head. He knew these bazaars very well. As per practice, these were his streets. Father would not even approach their shadows. Holding that waist-thread stick, he had to go to each and every house. What an irksome job!

Washing his face, eating the saddannam if it was there, he would set out in the morning only to return in the afternoon. Nothing was certain. Everything was at the mercy of the man above. If they did sell, they would sell well. Good meant two or three—otherwise death! No matter what, they would not get sold. Mother would say if the first buyer's hand is good, everything would go off smoothly. If one went by this, one had to assume that there were no good people. There were days when he returned empty-handed. That day would be worse than hell. Couldn't even sleep at night. Even if mother would not say anything, father would not keep quiet in his intoxicated condition. "Arey, if he can't even sell this much, how will he get by? Cha…cha." He would keep on talking till he slept off.

"Let him be. He's still young. Doesn't know his hands from his feet. Even this much is enough. Otherwise what should he do? Die?" Mother would try to pacify father. "I know about such people. You don't tell me anything. God knows where he sits and dozes. Will business come by just like that? He must beg at each and every house. He must convince them and make them buy. Doesn't he know that? Who will buy if you keep silent? He can't utter a word. Son of a whore who can't find a livelihood even if shown the way…if you see the way he's going, he doesn't seem one to stick on…" Father would keep on talking this way. Mother would say something for a while and keep quiet.

Those words would produce a fever in him. A tremor that would not stop. A deep fear that seemed to gnaw at his veins and go deep within him. Mother too would not argue forcefully on his behalf. He would swallow his sobs somewhere deep inside and go to sleep at some hour.

In fact, the pain he had suffered that day was not insignificant. He had set out that day as usual. He had gone about all the streets he had to every day. He had gone on streets he did not know and on those that were not his route. Though his feet were hurting and his eyes burning, the determination that he had to take something home did not leave him. But to no avail. Dispirited, he grew weak and returned home. Leave alone the fact that he was dying with misery that he was unable to sell anything, his father's words making light of his efforts were hurting him like knives being thrust into the mattress. Both pain and fear were ripping his heart. Mother too was keeping silent. He was unable to understand anything.

He didn't know when he went to sleep that night. By the time he got up in the morning, the little one had licked the vessel clean. He went to work that day on a starving stomach. Mother had asked him to buy and eat something with the first half-a-rupee he got. Though it was nearing noon, he neither got that half-a-rupee nor did his stomach get filled. He felt disgusted with his work. Wretched work! He felt that if he found another job he would not be put through such hardships. He felt that rather than this life, his previous life was better. But if they had stuck on to that village, by now they would have become corpses with pangs of hunger.

In a manner of speaking, they themselves were not responsible either for Rangadu's life or his father's life. When they used to be in their village, his father would do coolie work. Not bad. They did not have the misfortune of fasting. Didn't know how those days had deceived them. But even that work was not available anymore. Father had mortgaged his house, taken loans, drunk gruel or some such and carried on for a while. Soon there had been no sight of a job. Even those who had fields did not have enough work. Small-time farmers were leaving their houses, selling all that they had, and going to the town holding their stomachs in their hands. After the village people had said this and that, father had taken up this work.

There was a reason as to why father took up this work. The ancestors of mother and father had made a living with this work. Mother would keep talking about this now and again. It seemed that if her grandfather did not tie the waist-thread for a newborn, no child would have survived. They would lead their lives with "the luxuries of well-to-do people". Father too had done this work in his childhood! In fact he did not like getting into this once again. But he had no choice. It was only at mother's insistence.

After seeing his own experience and that of his father, Rangadu felt that his mother's words were just a bag of water. That she was a "big liar". He thought maybe that was why his father too had said those things. Okay! But father would also not try to find another job thinking that this one was not good enough to eke out a living.

Just like the tear on his shirt, father would not pay any attention to this work. He would go out. He would sell waist-threads if people bought them. He would spend half of what he got on arrack. He would behave as if he did not care what happened to his house, his wife and children. Mother too would never ask father to find another job. It seemed her stomach was filled just with his holding on to that waist-thread stick.

It had become a crow-like life. A wretched life. No village, no place gave them any surety. If they did not get business, move out, go to another place. Like this, there was no count of how many villages they had roamed about with those tattered mats, waist-thread sticks, woebegone faces and empty stomachs. He found people who bargained disgusting. If he said half-a-rupee, they would say a quarter! If he said a quarter, they would say ten paise! They would take his life out. They would not have the brains to think if it was even possible to survive on so little! Men too were like that. They would keep on bargaining. Moaning and groaning, with great difficulty they would give what they had to, as if they were doing it out of compassion!

The more he thought of it, the more disgusting he found it. Rather than live with this constant annoyance and irritation, Rangadu felt it was better to die. "Wretched people, wretched house! If they don't sell, give it up!" he thought. "Won't something work out?" he thought. He believed that other than this work, any other work would give happiness and bring money.

Again, hunger gnawed at his stomach.

The sun was scorching hot. He felt as if he was in a frying pan and being fried. As he kept walking, he neared the railway station. He went on to the other platform and collapsed on a bench under a tree. A few beggar families lived under that tree. The women, men and children were gulping down food and were talking animatedly amongst themselves. He was unable to make out what they were talking about. If one saw the way they were eating, even hunger would die away. Unable to look at them, he turned instead to look up at a monkey that was jumping about on the tree.

When he looked down again, he found two youngsters on the platform. Both of them were collecting paper, plastic and trash. Amidst all kinds of talk and songs, they were separating them and stacking them into piles. An old man who was watching them, and licking his fingers as he was eating, said something to them. Lifting the faded cap on his head a little and baring his teeth, one of the youngsters gave him a mocking reply. The old man left laughing.

"Look there...at that picture. I have to see her today," said the other youngster, pointing at a film poster on the wall. His friend looked at it, and laughed awkwardly. Rangadu too looked in that direction. But unwilling to look at the poster, he turned his head away.

Even as they kept talking they were doing their work briskly. Rangadu sat wide-eyed wondering what they were going to do. "What are all these for?" he finally managed to ask with great difficulty. They both muttered something and laughed at him mockingly. He did not understand what they had said. He thought of asking again but was unable to. They stuffed all the papers into a big sack and tied it up. Similarly they put all the bottles and the remaining trash into a plastic bag. Then heaving a big sigh of "Ammayya!" and taking out a beedi each from their pockets and putting it between thin black lips, they heaved the sack onto their heads, lifted the plastic bag in their hands, and set out. "We'll get more today than yesterday," they told each other. Rangadu kept looking at them. This job seemed doable. He also thought that it seemed like one that would bring in money.

Running towards them as they were walking away, Rangadu muttered with trembling lips, "I too want this job." "No work, no nothing...Go, go away!" growled one of the youngsters, as if he was the boss. "Let him come, poor thing," said the other one, feeling sorry, smiling as if he was God himself.

Turning many corners, they brought him to a place. Big sacks had been stacked up high. A big weighing balance. Only bamboo screens were the barriers. All of this was inside a hut. Papers lay scattered. Bottles. Iron things. Some youngsters were sitting in front of them and separating them.

"Ayyagaru! You asked us to look out for someone for grading. I have caught hold of this fellow." Pointing to Rangadu, the youngster said this to a man who was there. That man looked terrible and reeked of sweat. Time and again he would keep touching his moustaches. He looked at Rangadu and almost growled, "Well, will you work? Or will you scoot in two days' time?" Rangadu nodded his head slowly to indicate that he would work.

The man stood there weighing all the things that the youngsters brought, and looking into the accounts. After a while, he asked Rangadu, who was looking this way and that, perplexed, to come close to him. "Orey, idiot!" When he screamed out, one of the youngsters there came and stood near him. Without a shirt, dark in complexion, he looked like a log. That youngster looked proudly at Rangadu, took him along with him and started showing him what to do and how to do things. The work seemed easy enough. When the youngster thought Rangadu was not paying attention and that his eyes were wandering, he did not hesitate to beat him. Rangadu did not take long to note that except for their appearance, there wasn't much difference between this youngster and the owner.

The two days that he spent there disturbed him greatly. As if he had fallen from the frying pan into the fire. The few rupees he earned each day got spent in different ways. Eating something. Sleeping right there. Though the stupid youngster also slept there, he would do so at a distance. He would get Rangadu to sweep, make him roll out the mattress and sleep right royally. He was the one who had got the certificate of good conduct from the owner. As the work had increased, the owner employed Rangadu. When Rangadu who was perplexed about the business from the time that he joined work asked the youngster about it, the youngster got angry. When somebody said it would be sent to the company, he said, "Okay," and remained silent thereafter.

The owner showed his cruelty on the second day itself, saying Rangadu was not doing his job well. He came to understand that this too was not a comfortable job. That youngster was like "the pestle on the infected toe nail". Rangadu joining the job gave the youngster a lot of comfort.

Remaining here has become very difficult. The thought that he has to somehow get out of their iron grip is not allowing him to breathe easily. In the meanwhile, he has finished sweeping. He takes the broom, keeps it in a corner, stands for a while, heaves a sigh like one who has come to a decision, and cuts off his train of thoughts.

When he rubs his eyes and looks, the darkness is just receding. People have started to move about on the road. The stupid youngster is still sleeping. Rangadu's eyes are hurting. He hasn't slept the whole night. For some reason or the other, he hadn't been able to sleep.

Rangadu comes out onto the road. He is extremely exhausted. But with every step he takes forward, happiness is starting to build its nest in his heart. The disgust that has been accumulated over the last four days is slowly disappearing. The thought that he would live as before is enthusing the blood in his veins. How blissfully he would sleep! He would be beaten only once in a while. Mother would be overwhelmed with happiness to see him. Sister would have forgotten all that had happened. She would be overwhelmed with happiness and would bring all her earnings and throw them in front of him. Father would not bother about anything.

Dawn is slowly breaking. He is walking briskly. The pain... the fear...that had crushed his heart are receding. With darkness fading away, the shadow of the sun is spreading. The mild sun is driving away all the hopelessness, the darkness, the pain, the tremor and the weakness that had engulfed each atom of his body.

He walks all the way home, full of happiness, excitement, anticipation...But, when he reaches the place, he feels as if a thunderbolt has struck him and he is unable to move his feet and hands. He cannot believe what he sees...Ground that has been smoothened because people lived there...Ash on the stone stove that has been left behind after being blown away by the wind... Unable to utter a word, he involuntarily takes a step backward.

Then, like one crazed, he starts running back on the very road on which he had come.

The lone stump of a tree trunk watches him silently, pitifully.

Originally published in Telugu as 'Adivi'
in *Andhra Jyothy Sachitravara Patrika*, 27 May 1983, pp. 100–110.

8. In the Intermittent Rains...

"You have been able to capture the colours of these ruins quite well. But I don't know how you caught those colours so accurately on the canvas and what you mixed! In each painting, the coloured bodies of the women in striking contrast to the ruins...that cloud...As far as I know, hasn't this been your canvas for the last ten years?" she said, looking keenly into the canvas once again.

She knew that timeline better than him. Wasn't it only ten years ago that he felt there was nothing more left for him in the village after father passed away? She had called him and made him come to Hyderabad along with mother, on the pretext of a job that he was forced to take up.

He had tried to love this city several times. But each time he had tried, Hyderabad would produce something dramatic for him to hate it.

Just as he had begun to feel confident that he was settling down, the city swallowed his mother.

Was he attributing his helplessness to the city then? Perhaps! He never dug out the reasons. That the fear of living had increased more than before was indeed true. His helplessness too was real. A truth he knew very well. The fear that if he took one false step, his life might be shattered. Love and marriage with her too were, right? Just a few failed steps. Little or no faith in his job. Uncertain as to what the next moment would bring...Unable to live in this moment.

"Why are you so terrified of everything? You didn't have this much fear in you when you were in the village, right?" mother would say. He did not have an answer, but perhaps mother knew what he really was.

"You are hiding something under these ruins."

She said this after peering into the canvas possibly for the fourth time.

She knew the exact distance from which a painting would appear close. When she stood before it in that manner, she seemed to become a part of the painting, and he felt as if a violet flower that he had forgotten had bloomed on the canvas just then.

"Are you thinking of what to say? Or are you lost in imagining another painting?"

He wanted to laugh as usual and keep quiet, but she would not let him.

"Yes. No one examines my work as keenly as you do...you alone know it well."

"No, in fact even I don't know. I'm only telling you what I see. But I feel there is something behind every painting that I do not see. There definitely must be."

"Well...I don't know if there is! I wouldn't know. My work is done once I have drawn the picture, right?"

"Until you speak in a different language, I won't be able to understand your colours and lines. I must have seen this painting at least ten times, from ten different directions. But, I am still unable to find you in it."

"Colours and lines are alone its language. If it is not understood in that language, it means that the painting has failed! Even so, let me ask you something. Why should you find me in it?"

"I don't know why. But I have been thinking for the past ten years that it would be good if I could find a little bit of you in your paintings. When did I first see your painting? How was I then? How am I now? If we think about all this, as far as you are concerned, I am just the same as I was when we met in Intermediate for the first time. Not knowing you, even when I know you, I am unable to believe that I really do know you."

How was it possible for her to have remembrances of something long past? He didn't like to remember. He was afraid of memories.

"Can't say."

"Is that so? Are you now sliding into silence? No, no, babu!"

That impish smile that lit up her face.

Sometimes she would say, "You must become a full-time artist. Working in this newspaper, suddenly getting up from sleep in the afternoon, getting ready and leaving...drawing something there...I feel that this is not your life. And then the daily fears of a job, their likes and dislikes..."

"Ammo, don't say such things! There is no stability for anyone doing anything full-time here. It's enough just to have the dregs." The job was not more important than her. But he could not leave the job he disliked as easily as she had left him who she loved a lot.

She would come for a while like that and go away. A love of five or six years. Two years of marriage. Then separation. How many uncertainties in those two years...An added fear that she might become pregnant. The two of them knew that that was not the only reason for their separation.

According to what they had agreed upon, the two of them would not discuss things like re-marriage or children. After separation they thought that their lives must not remain like a broken bond. So they had simply banned those mundane matters from conversation! They wanted to spend the short time that they had together happily, and look forward to more such times. That was it! Up to this point, the agreement had not been breached.

For the short time that she was there, he would breathe happily, and even after she left her laugh would resonate in his room. He wanted only that much. Perhaps she too did. Perhaps that is why, even after the second marriage, she had of her own volition not let go of his friendship. What if she had...? He did not know! Some thoughts were difficult to bear.

"Don't go," he would feel like telling her sometimes. But till that moment, he had never stopped anyone on his own. Not those who came, nor those who left. How many times had she come and gone.

In fact, perhaps it was his unambiguous silence that sent her back each time!

Why was he like that? Such passivity terrified him sometimes. He could not remember what he had asked from life the first time that he had met her.

As she said, "the daily fears" were in fact true, but perhaps these fears were there in him even before he came to this city, to this job. They might have grown after coming to Hyderabad. Primarily, it was fear born out of the disbelief of people, of friendships, of getting together. More than all these, the all encompassing fear that he himself had created.

Once, he had written down the list of all these fears in his diary. First fear: That this life would not give him anything; it pretended to give but took away father. Three days after he was absolutely sure that he had brought back father as he had recovered, he passed away in his sleep. Just like that, mother who was as dear as life—till the last moment, he could not imagine being motherless.

Second fear: That these friendships and bonds, as they become closer, become distant and torment all the more. Who among those from his childhood had remained with him? Those he had thought had become very close, how ruthlessly they all had gone away! In different ways—some due to death, some to live in faraway countries, some due to enmity without reason.

And now the third, his present greatest and most important fear: That the nearer she came, she too would go that much further away, and that he would never be prepared for that distance!

When she came into his life for the first time, he had just stumbled upon the secret of colours. He had stopped writing poems then, and started hiding in colours. When...even when he was in Intermediate...wasn't that so?

That was indeed hiding!

She had been the same since then. He knew very well that he was not the same. She did not know how to hide. She would say whatever she wanted to say. It seemed as if she was living in two different worlds. He too would feel like telling her everything. That in fact his was a life where there was nothing to say. He had stopped writing poems after he had lost faith in words and other things. It seemed as if he had decided that there was nothing more to say with those words.

She would come again today.

He would feel like cleaning that solitary room all the more for her. Those books that were strewn around haphazardly, the bed sheets and pillows on the bed, the mess in the kitchen...the dust on the dressing table he did not know why he had bought...he would feel like cleaning everything and having a bath and sitting and waiting.

She would come in a while. The fragrance she brought, the beguiling smiles, some conversation...he wanted them always! She would come today in a little while. Those too would come with her. Would go away. After that, he and the ruins of his paintings.

Initially she would come like that in the last summer holidays of Intermediate.

Van Gogh's biography, *Lust for Life* is what she got him that summer! After that she would bring him something or the other. She was the one always giving! Till date, he had never given her anything. Even in marriage.

She did not ask for anything either. Except for a few questions!

He remembered quite clearly the number of questions she had asked and the number of responses he had given.

Mother kept hoping till the very end that they would be united once again in marriage. "When the two of you are together, you look very happy, ra!" she would say. Mother said the same thing in front of her too.

"Perhaps there isn't so much happiness in being together, amma..." When he had said this later, mother almost hit him.

She had been like this for the past ten years. She seemed like one in a dream. Did she too have fears like him? He didn't know. Didn't even feel like asking her. It wasn't just fear. Wouldn't both feel that the mystery in this friendship would be lost?

One evening after she had come and gone, opening the diary, he had felt like writing something. But he had not written. Had been unable to write. Throwing away the diary, leaning back in the chair, he had remained just like that. That night, he had painted another scene of ruins. A woman walking through some ruins, towards high crumbling walls...without showing her face to the world!

Amidst the colours of the ruins, she in a green saree...the contrast of the two colours had always haunted him.

That day there had been a matter that she had hidden from him. Almost bringing it to her lips but not desiring the discussion around it, she had stopped.

"More than the uncertainty in a marital relationship, the bond that is continuing like this—the uncertainty of bonds with no hopes or aspirations was better. To me, the restraints of a marital bond look like the colours of these ruins you are creating there."

The last day when they had taken her to the hospital, mother too had been in the same green saree. When he had dropped her at the hospital and was going to the office, mother had smiled happily. Had smiled very contentedly, very freely. Mother would always smile like that, but that morning, he had not wanted to leave that smile and go.

He had felt like staying on with mother. Just then, the phone call, saying, "You're coming to work, aren't you? Today's the deadline! Don't forget." The word "No" had come to the tip of his tongue. Why had he not been able to say it?

He ought to have stayed on with mother—then he would have heard her last words. "Ask him to look after himself carefully, amma!" It seemed that after making the nurse promise to say this, mother had passed away. There was pity in the nurse's eyes as she was telling him this. Mother...!

That evening mother had gone away. After that his relationship with the world had snapped. Before his life in Hyderabad, he had never known what fear was!

"You go about those ruined hills and forts all by yourself even after it is dark! Why? Can't you be at home happily?"

He would recall mother's warning all the time.

The high walls of the fort were indeed his obsession. Even more, the hills that lay between those walls. One evening by the time he had returned home it was pitch dark. He did not know for how long he had sat on the hill inside the fort, nor remembered what he had been thinking. By the time he had realised and got his bearings, it was night, and he felt scared. He had started climbing down the steps of the fort quickly. The steps were very wide. He had no fear of falling as he descended them. Some steps were smooth. In that darkness a little moonlight fell on them, making them look wet. In his eagerness and hurry to get back home quickly, on the very last step, he slipped and fell.

He wasn't hurt very badly. But that day, mother had been more frightened than him. To her, his fall had appeared as a sign of his future life.

"Don't go alone anywhere! I cannot take care of you. I don't know how to teach you caution and fear!" Saying this, mother had shed tears.

Would it have been different if his father were alive?

He too, like his father! The question whether he too would go away somewhere with death like his father would have haunted mother. But mother would not make her fears so obvious. As she had yearned that her son should know only courage, she had shielded him like the eyelids the eye, so that even the thought of his father's absence would not affect him. It wasn't as if he doubted that, in order to fill the emptiness after father's sudden death, she had gradually increased her affection for him.

Such a mother, bold and outwardly strong perhaps, had turned to ruins within herself! In her last days, she had developed a certain weakness, a numbness.

He would never be able to forget the brightness in mother's eyes when he had given her the earnings received from the sale of his first painting.

At that moment, he had thought he would like to see more of such brightness! At the same time he had also felt anxious. That a time would come when his paintings too would go away from him—that nothing and no one would remain with him! That ultimately everything...everyone had to go away!

Now, his fear about her too was the same! The nearer she grew, the more his fear, the more his insecurity that she too would go far away. Later, when she grew closer still, he feared the emptiness if either of them should depart, for whatever reason—that emptiness was a great fear!

He had a vision in his dream that morning and was holding on to it. The same fort...a slight drizzle. When it drizzled on those stone ruins the colours looked wonderful! He wanted to capture those colours on the canvas. Through the drizzle, a moving shadow—she.

The same dream. He wanted the same colours.

Her coming and going. Not just in the dream. Just like in the dream she would come once a month. On the day she would come—a spark, a brightness, a movement in his solitary, still life.

He had never voiced, never expressed that he wanted something more than this.

She too had never expected that he would ask. He had never asked her if she had married again, if she had children or even what she did or what she did not do.

She would come, stay a little while. Some conversation. More of silence. If possible, tea! That is all.

He got up from bed and stood in front of the mirror.

In the mirror, a shadow moved—she.

Wasn't it his belief that she…she alone was real?

Wasn't it so?

Originally published in Telugu as 'Vachche Poye Vanallo…' in *Aadivaram Andhra Jyothy*, 8 October 2018, pp. 111–119.

9. Telangi Patta

"Abba...ye hamara gaon nai! Father, this is not our village!"

I felt as if someone had whipped my body as I was tossing and turning, unable to sleep.

Was it Munna's voice?

I looked to my side. On the other side of the bed, Razia was fast sleep. Having erased all the commotion and vexation of the morning, she was sleeping very peacefully.

Munna, who was sleeping in the middle of the cot, was uneasily tossing and turning like me.

Earlier, when he used to sleep, a tiny smile would blossom on his lips, spreading to the entire face, and a great beauty would bloom on his tender face. That bud would touch my inner thoughts and wounds softly and coolly like the waft of a breeze, and all my inner turmoil would be blown away somewhere.

There was no smile on his face now.

It was as if he was hiding some tumult that he could not express and, unable to withhold it, was feeling restless, just like the hell I was going through, unable to sleep...

A month ago...

I had just returned from the shoe shop. As I was about to go in and wash my feet and hands, Munna came running from behind and held me tight with both his hands.

"Abba...today Seenu did not play with me! It seems he won't play with me anymore!" he said, sobbing.

In the meanwhile Razia had come out, shouting, "It doesn't matter if Seenu doesn't play with you! I will bring Javed over tomorrow, and you and he can play for as long as you wish to!" But Munna would not listen.

Seenu was his dost, his dear friend. He too liked Munna a lot.

I could not understand what had happened.

"What happened? The two of you always played together every day, right...? Then what happened now?"

"It seems his mother has asked him not to," said Razia.

"Why so?" I had asked, turning towards her.

"Kya mareki! How the hell do I know why!" Razia had said, not wanting to discuss it any further.

"You tell me, Munna," I had said, drawing him close.

He had come and sat on my lap. "Abba! Seenu also scolded me today."

"What did he say?"

"That I was a bad boy."

Razia had then intervened again, saying, "What...! Do you have to play only with *him*? Are there no other children for you to play with? Javed, Rabia, Rehana, Sajid...?"

"But what has happened?" No matter how hard I tried, I was unable to think beyond their play-world.

"Why do you speak as if you don't know anything? Our child alone goes there eagerly jumping about, but those children don't even come near the shadow of our house."

"Is that true?"

"My misfortune! You don't pay attention to anything I say! I just don't understand! Didn't I tell you...that we should take a house only in the khila? Did you listen to me? You are just a Telangi patta!"[1]

"Do you have to say that?" I had almost screamed at her in anger. "For everything...it's always just that!"

"But isn't it true? Have you ever been a Musalman? Just think!" Saying this, Razia had gone off into the kitchen.

"That is okay...But now tell me about Munna," I had said, following her.

---

[1]**Telangi patta:** literally 'Telugu leaf', a reference, usually derogatory, to Muslims in Telangana who speak only Telugu.

"What is there to tell? If we stay on here a little longer, he will be left neither here nor there! No Hindu children will play with him. And if he goes to the khila after he grows up a bit, they won't let him in," Razia had said.

I had been lost in thought.

Khila...khila! I had been haunted by it ever since I came to this town!

Seventy five per cent of the houses of Musalmans in the town were inside the fort. For that matter, it was said, "Only those who live inside the khila are real Musalmans." I had heard this even when I was in our village. After mother died, I did not feel like living in that village anymore. There was nothing I could do in that village. It had also become difficult to pull along with the little I got from the paan-dabba stall near the station. I would pass away my time sitting in the stall, reading the unsold Telugu newspaper.

Except for Ahmed saab who came now and then from the town, I had no other relatives. Ahmed saab too was my relative from Razia's side, not mine; he was Razia's maternal uncle. As for the relatives I had, there was Usman who used to idle away his hours at the station, Sitaram who had studied tenth with me and failed, and who would open his barber's stall whenever he felt like, and Satyam who had nothing to do but sit at the tea stall discussing politics! Razia would keep scolding me, "That entire batch of idlers is forever hovering around you!" The four or five relatives I had were all Telangis. She never considered Usman a human being. So, even though he was a Muslim, he was not counted as one. In the same way, my village too had labelled me a "Telangi patta".

As long as I lived in the village, whenever things were beyond me and my capacity, or there was nothing in the house to sustain us, she would say, "Telangi patta!" After coming to the town, a sentence was added to this abuse. No matter what went amiss, she would say, "Didn't I tell you...if we were in the khila such a thing would not have happened?" I would hear this at least ten times every day.

I did not come to this town of my own accord. It must be said that it was Razia's mamu Ahmed saab who had dragged us here.

In the village, one day I had been sitting in my paan-dabba and was reading the unsold Telugu newspaper as usual when Ahmed saab appeared out of nowhere, saying, "Janab! Ye Telangi chhodo, Urdu akhbar padho! Give up this Telugu mister, and read the Urdu newspaper!"

When I had folded the paper and hung it on the stand, Ahmed saab had begun to speak in his typical manner, saying, "How long will you while away your time here with makkhi-machchar, flies and mosquitoes? Come to the town. You can get work in some shop there."

"What can I do there?"

"Whatever you do in the town, a little bit of money will fall into your hands. There, all the people are our own, right?" he had said, straightening and smoothening his beard to his heart's content as he talked.

What he meant by "our people" was clear to me. But I had been doubtful about his "our" people also being close to me. I had studied a bit of Urdu and Arabic. Even though initially I had followed the panchgana five times prayer, the namaz and ada prayers for fulfillment five times every day, in their view, I was not pak, not a pure Musalman. In fact they suspected that I had become one with the Telangis.

They would draw mother close, calling her "Gorima". But they would always look at me as an outsider. In fact, there had been no one who was concerned about our family after father passed away. When the relatives had snatched away what little land we had, those who were close relatives also tried to take away the roof, that was about to collapse anytime! But mother had not let it collapse. With that, they had begun to call mother, "stubborn Gorima!" After that entire business, I had begun to feel disgusted about relatives and all those so called "our people".

Mother had taught me Urdu and Arabic and made me come up to this level. But our lives went by wondering if we would be able to survive that day or not. With father's death and the burden of the household falling on me, my education had taken a beating. The huge debt that had been incurred for younger sister's wedding remained. There had been no one who had stood by me in this entire battle of life. That I could manage to have this pan-dabba had been possible only because my Telangi dosts had given money and such.

So where then was the surprise of my becoming a Telangi patta!

"Gorima! You survive from fazar to isha[2] namaz on Urdu and Arabic. But your boy is forever roaming around with Telangi boys." Everyone would say this to mother's face. Mother too had tried many times to persuade me.

"Why can't you go around with our people instead?" she would say.

"Who are *our* people?" When I would question her in this manner, she would not know what to say. "Mere pet me ek Telangi patta nikla! I have given birth to a Telangi patta!" Feeling bad, she would keep quiet.

Along with this, a great change had come about in me because of my association with Satyam. A number of people would come to Satyam's house from the town. Though I did not know who they were, my small brain had understood that they were all very well educated and that all of them were very angry with the world. After spending some time with Satyam, the bearded man's books in Satyam's hands had attracted me. When I had brought those books home and was reading them, mother would look at them suspiciously and say, "Yera…why don't you polish the little Urdu and Arabic you know! Why that bearded man now?"

It must have appeared as if I was really reading those books, but in fact I was unable to comprehend even a word! When I had asked Satyam why this was so, he said, "Do you have to understand everything? Ask your people to explain one tiny bit of what they

---

[2]**fazar to isha:** fazar (dawn prayer), dhuhr or zuhar (noon prayer), asar (late afternoon prayer), maghrib (sunset prayer) and isha namaz (night prayer), the five daily prayers followed by Muslims.

study from fazar to isha. Our people read mantras for everything, right...have they understood even one of them?"

True. But this bearded man's books had some magic. It was as if a torch light had suddenly been flashed on some discontent hidden deep within me. My Razia did not recognise any language in the world other than Urdu and Arabic. The minute she spotted the Telugu alphabet anywhere, that was it! She would get so anxious she would start worrying that we would all go to hell that very moment! For such a person, when I persisted in bringing home just those Telugu books, her anger and pain knew no end. She would even think that the poverty at home was all because of these Telugu books. If I hung Telugu newspapers in the paan-dabba, she would curse me, saying, "When I tell you that as long as those kafir hurp, those devilish infidel letters are there, your paan-dabba will never run properly, you don't listen!"

Perhaps I might indeed have become a "Telangi patta". I would not deny it.

Was I not a Musalman? I would not be able to say yes.

Razia saying this of me was nothing new. But now it appeared new. Similarly, Razia saying we ought to live inside the khila too was not new. But now it seemed very new. Why did Munna need all these problems? What was happening in his little world? I could not sleep.

Was I living in some dream? True. All these days, Munna was unaware of these problems. Razia and Ahmed saab had looked at many houses inside the khila. I found one reason or the other to reject them. But the most important reason was that I abhorred walls. I found it more abhorrent to live behind high walls. No one knew the time period of this khila. But I felt that life within these walls was like bandeekhana, imprisonment. The malik of the shoe shop I worked in also lived inside the khila.

"Take a house inside the khila. If they are here, they will have Deeni malumaat, an Islamic education and true knowledge of our religion. There is also safety here for women," he had said just two days after I had joined work. Unable to refuse him, I had gone to the khila once and taken a look inside. One main entrance, high walls all around. The minute I had entered the khila, I wondered, "Am I in a different world?" The houses and the people there had appeared alien.

The environment of my village that I had been accustomed to had not been there. Burkhas were not new to me. Topis were not new to me. Beards were not new to me. Mother would always be in a burkha. Razia would not go out without a burkha even now. Father had never had a beard, but bearded people would visit our house a lot when we were in the village. Every Friday, father and I would wear topis and recite the Jumme ki namaz. But what did I find here? This was a totally new world. It had seemed to me that here any man without a beard was given piercing looks. But someone looking suspiciously at me had been new to me. Had been irritating. I had felt that I could not live within these walls even for a moment. I had come out of the khila immediately. Ammayya!...I had felt so relieved! There had been a breeze and my body had felt light.

I felt it would be better to live anywhere outside rather than be imprisoned out in the open. I had to anyway walk a long distance to go to the shop. Getting houses around Station Bazar was extremely difficult. So I had thought that it would be good to take a house close to Munna's school at least. I had found a small house for rent in Mamillagudem.

When I had told Ahmed saab this, he had twisted his face three fold.

"Bole to nai sunte ba, tum! You don't listen no matter what we say, my son! If you don't like the khila, leave it. Couldn't you find another Musalman locality in this big town?" he had said.

"I searched everywhere. There are Musalmans even in this Mamillagudem. Moreover, it's very close to Munna's school."

"Does Munna need only Telugu and English education, and not our education?"

"We teach that anyway at home, don't we?"

"No matter what you say, there should be apne log, apna mahol, our people, our milieu around us. Otherwise, it will be a problem!" Saying this, he had shown two or three more houses.

But I had not liked them much. Having finalised the Mamillagudem house, I had brought Razia and Munna to the town. But from the day they had arrived, Razia would find one reason or another to complain and would trouble me constantly by asking us to move into the khila. But I had felt that I ought to be firm about this. The reasons that either Razia or Ahmed saab gave had not seemed proper to me.

Now Razia seemed to have found a good opportunity to justify them.

It was a week since Babri Masjid had been demolished.

Though I would get irritated with her and say, "If a masjid is demolished somewhere else, what is the problem in living here?" she would not listen. Every day she would sit in front of the TV and keenly watch all those troubles unfold on it without blinking. "Dekho…look how they have demolished it! When I see his soorat, his face, I get so angry!" She meant P. V. Narasimha Rao. "He seems to have been aware of things…it was all pre-planned. All of them are one. Here, we alone are the outsiders. But no matter what I say, you just refuse to understand!"

From that afternoon, Razia would not step outside. "You have brought us here and thrown us amidst these brambles. I'm scared to death even to put a foot outside. Will they keep quiet when they see a burkha?"

"Then…why don't you remove the burkha and go out?"

"Aa…I'll also put on a bottu and go! Ever since the masjid has been demolished, each one is going around fakhar, proudly wearing a rupee-sized bottu!" She said this angrily and went in.

This change in her was very surprising!

Razia had never seen the people around her as outsiders. Neither did she look upon them as close ones. That was another matter. But today she was noticing their demeanour, their language, their dress and their bottu very closely. She was not just noticing them, they appeared to her to be part of a "conspiracy".

Why was I not feeling anything? Had Muslimness died within me? Perhaps!

Demolishing the masjid was indeed unjust. But so many things happening just because of that masjid...I felt that all these were more unjust than the demolition. Moreover, that was not a masjid where people did namaz on a daily basis. When I said this to Razia, she aimed the arrow at me again, saying, "People like you don't do namaz except on festival days. In a little while, all the masjids in the country will turn to ruins like that. They will demolish all of them and build temples and such in their place!"

But what was it to me if things happened to masjids and temples and such? First I had to think about Munna.

By the time I came back in the evening, Munna was playing at home.

As soon as I came, I washed my feet and hands, and started playing with Munna.

It was he who started speaking, "Today too Seenu did not play with me."

"What happened?"

"It seems we belong to Pakistan. Is that so, abba?"

"No, that is not so. Pakistan is not ours."

Just then Razia came rushing into the front room and said, "What do you know what is pak and what is not!"

"Where we are is pak," I said.

"Yes! Those big, big bottus, those stone gods...demolishing masjids and building temples in their place...all this is indeed pak for you!"

"Razia...not in front of the boy!"

"He knows all this better than you!" Saying so, Razia got ready for the evening namaz.

I drew Munna close.

"Abba, do we have to go to Pakistan?"

"Who said so?"

"Seenu said so the other day. Today Balu also said so."

"They don't know anything."

"Then why are we here, abba? Let's go to our village."

"Okay...let's see! Let's play something for a while," I said, trying to distract him. But it seemed that he would not be distracted. He followed his mother and went and stood near Razia who was doing her namaz.

I did not have the capacity to convince him. Because I did not have the power to explain something to him that was not clear even to myself. Razia had a kind of clarity. There was a distinct line that she drew between our people and people not our own. She would stand on that line and speak out whatever she wished to.

I was unable to say anything. For the first time, there was a conflict within me about my education and my knowledge of the world.

Yes...who was I? Why was I not as upset as Razia at the demolition of the masjid? Even Munna could see the difference in the people around us. Why was I unable to perceive it then? What did those who spoke to me and those whom I spoke to think about the demolition of the masjid? Satyam was not here. Seetaramulu was not here. Here, the only person I spoke to was Ahmed saab. But, I did not have much respect for his opinion.

More than the demolition of the masjid, what bothered me most was that Munna did not have anyone to play with.

Yes...perhaps I needed to learn to look at those around us from Munna's perspective!

I did not interact with them much. If they said "Namaskaram" I would reply "Namaskaram" and if they said "Salam" I would reply "Valekum salam". I would keep a distance from everyone in this town.

I did not have close relationships with any of them—nor did any relationships develop.

Razia was better than me in this respect. Neighbours who would come to ask for sugar, vegetable cart vendors, people she met at the water pump, Muslim women who would come to meet her—her world was larger than mine.

I would read the newspaper. I would fold the paper, tuck it under my arm and go to the shop. There wouldn't be a moment of leisure there. There would be customers till eight at night. Maliksaab... namaz five times a day...talking to all those who visited...sitting at the cash desk...the entire work was on me alone. I knew only a few words.

"What size?"

"Keep your foot there, saab."

"This will last long, saar."

"What colour?"

"This colour is in vogue now, madam."

These were the words I used every day.

Other than these I also knew a few words from the Telugu newspaper. But where did I have the time to read the paper? When I would be about to open the paper, Ahmed saab, saying, "*Siasat* dekho, bhai! Read *Siasat*, bhai!" would give me the Urdu paper.

If I were to read the paper on coming back home, my mind would not be on it. Play with Munna for a while, and then bed. I felt that my universe had become constricted now and shrunk.

I did not even know the universe that Munna knew.

When I went to bed with those very thoughts, it was ten!

Razia was sleeping. Munna was tossing and turning.

I went to lie down next to him. He clung to me immediately. I straightened the tresses on his forehead.

"Abba...ye hamara gaon nai! Abba, this is not our village!" he was saying.

I silently wept. True...but, what was our village? I drew him close.

"Let's go to our village."

Yes...but, which village was ours? What was there in the village that we left behind? Wasn't it the same there too? I thought that in this town there were at least a few who did not know our religion or our caste. Wasn't it the same here too? So, where should we go now?

"Pakistan...nee pilaka peekestan! Pakistan...I will pull out your pigtail!" Munna was talking in his sleep.

"I am no one. I cannot go anywhere...I am a Telangi patta."

Yes, that's true! I was lost in thought.

That night I could not sleep at all.

Originally published in Telugu as 'Telangi Patta' in *Vaartha Aadivaram Anubandham*, 1 May 2005, pp. 120–131.

10. Dhedee

Mirror in front.

Without meaning to, I see myself.

Is that me? Is the one I am seeing me? No. Not at all. Isn't it Usman? Yes. It is Usman. Yes, it is he with his dirty clothes, his stringy beard, always parading his pitiable state in a stately manner with a baton like a magic wand. Yes. Why do I look like Usman? I feel like spitting on that image. Why? Do I appear outside as I appear in the mirror? In fact, how has he entered my body and my brain?

"Razia…?"

"Aa," she turns irritated, even as she sleeps.

"Who am I?"

"Aa…?" She is perplexed.

"Aziz beta, bolo, tell me."

"Baba."

"Nasreen, tell me."

"Baba."

They do not understand my question.

Now, at this moment, from their point of view, I am a madman. They look quizzically at their mother. Her eyes well up at my condition. She covers her face with her pallu and goes in. Razia does not say anything more than that.

What if I ask Ramdas?

"Arey Ramdas! Tell me, who am I?"

I come out screaming.

Where should I run?

I cannot say anything. If I think, things churn in my stomach. I do not know in what way I am different from Usman. Perhaps he is better than me! I have lost even the small job I had. At home, a wife and two children wait. I am afraid to walk in the streets with my head held high. I am angry with my pyjama and my lalchi. I am irritated with the Muslimness evident on my face.

Who am I?

Why don't I have the opportunity to earn a few chips like everyone else and take care of my family? Ramdas says, "Let it be, bhai. You, sister-in-law and the children come and live with me. We'll give you whatever we eat." But, it doesn't feel right. Even if I agree, will Razia keep quiet? If we had to depend on others, we would have somehow got on in the village itself. Why like this, having come so far from everyone to the town? Ramdas, who had come along with me, sits outside the shoe shop I worked in, repairs shoes, and somehow fills his stomach. He is pulling along with his family.

I am the one who has not fitted in anywhere. I have no work. He has work. That's the difference!

Sometimes I think, if only I were to learn his trade and sit on the road side, life would get by somehow! What's wrong in that? The day has to get by.

But something comes in the way.

Usman haunts me not only in my dreams, but even in reality.

That game seems to be going on still at the village square. Even if I recall it now, how disgusting it seems. For the entire village, Usman is a toy. If he goes to the Kamma street, they tie palm leaves to his ears. In the Brahmin street, he is a used leaf-plate. Saying chhee-chhee they shove him off openly. If he goes to the wada, outside the village, he is an untouchable to everyone. In the ooru, the village proper, no matter where he goes, his life is just that. But how different he would be with mother! Not acting crazy, but behaving well. Mother too would look at him not as a crazy person, but as a human being. When everyone else would repulse him, Usman would come crying to our house. Mother would say a few kind words to him, and give him a cup of tea. With that, he would become normal again.

But whenever I looked at him I would feel disgusted. Even on a festival day, he would wash and wear that same dirty pyjama and lalchi. If he were either next to me or in the opposite row during namaz, that dirty stench would hit my nostrils.

But now his pure heart beneath those dirty clothes touches me. My hunger-filled life, my present torn pyjama and lalchi, the looks people give me…

It seems to me as if Usman led a more dignified life then than I do now.

It's true!

This is not of now. It is as if a fire lit within a long time ago is blazing now. Just as in my childhood when mother would sit in front of the stove and blow "usoo, usoo" through a smoke pipe, and the fire under the pot would blaze all of a sudden, I would remember something and suddenly my entire body, as if perplexed, would boil like maize-rice. If I do not think of the stove, the pot, the maize-rice, and Usman along with them, it is as if all that I ate would be insect ridden.

When I recall how upset mother would become if she could not get maize by the afternoon, I feel totally drained. Then, when that crazy Usman would go pluck maize from somewhere, hold her chin and plead, "Gorima, mai nai dekh sakta, ye leke bachcheko zara khilao. Gorima, I can't bear to see this, here, take this and feed the children," how many times did I not see tears roll down tup, tup from mother's eyes like tender maize.

As for me, just seeing Usmangadu would make my stomach churn. "Amma, ye galeez nakko, mai leke aaton. Amma, I don't want this filthy thing. I'll go get some." Saying this, I would look him up and down, at his dirty clothes and his wretched appearance, and quickly go out of the house. But who would give me maize? Would Sarojinammagaru give? Would the teacher give? Thinking that they might, I would go to the houses of Sarojinammagaru and the teacher. They would speak to me nicely and smilingly ask, "What is it, babu?"

But would there be maize in their houses? They eat white paddy rice—shining white like jasmine. My mouth would water looking at that rice with dal or pieces of avakaya pickle. It seems white rice used to be cooked in our house too when father was alive. After father passed away, maize-rice, millet-rice, we would boil whatever grain we could lay our hands on and eat. Sometimes we would not get even that.

"Yera, why don't you study?" Saying this, the teacher would keep a banana in my hand.

"Why will he study? He will roam around bekar, jobless, just like this deewana, crazy Usman! Will these Muslims ever be able to pronounce words properly? Are they stable?" Saying this, Sarojinamma would laugh out loud.

I would not get angry with them. I would get angry with Usmangadu.

Thhoo! You are belittling the dignity of Muslims, aren't you? I would think to myself.

I would think that I would never ever want a dog's life like Usman's. After eating the banana when I would get going, Usmangadu would again look at me as if he was looking at an insect and laugh, saying, "Kya babuji?" That was like chilli powder on my wounds! Kicking the dust with my feet in vexation, I would go home. "Babu, kidar gaya ba? Where did you go?" mother would say, and bring some maize-rice and gongura chutney. When one with burning hunger ate the morsels mother had mixed, would the world remain visible? At that moment there was no Usmangadu, nor his stringy beard, nor his dirty shirt. Only heaven would float in the stomach then!

I would sit on a big boulder outside the masjid after namaz in the evening. Otherwise, I would romp around with the boys. Unable to bear the noise, Hazrat saab, caressing his beard, would come and scold me a lot.

"Kya, bey? Ammee ke kaam me zara haath bata. Aisa bandar ke jaisa kyo nachta? Ja…ja…! What, bey? Go help your ammee with her work. Why do you jump around like a monkey? Go… go…!" And he would chase me away.

At that time, Usmangadu would argue on my behalf.

To tell the truth, all the older people sitting on the boulder would tease Usmangadu. I would find such play disgusting. Abusing him thoroughly, they would make fun of his beard and clothes. His manner would seem to suggest that he was born in this village only to put up with all this. No matter what anyone would say, he would give his crazy laugh.

That's it! I find that laugh disgusting!

Usman has burst out laughing.

Looking at me now…looking at the empty stomachs of both my children…looking at my wife's irritation and her unbearable patience…

When Malik saab called me one day and sent me away saying, "Tere se kaam nai hota…doosra rasta dekhlo. You can't do the work, find another job," didn't I too come out laughing just like him—like a madman? How many jobs did I have to do to take care of my family!

If I go to Ramdas, he says, "How can you do this work…?"

Ramdas is completely immersed in his work.

True. I can't do anything. The Arabic mother taught me cannot feed me even for a day. I am extremely fond of Arabic. Mother taught me alif, laam, meem perhaps, but it is with my own efforts that I was able to read the Quran. How she loved that! Forgetting all her trials and tribulations, she would be lost in listening to my musical recitation of the Quran. I would find much peace reading it out like that…as if butter was being delicately smeared on a wound. I thought that I would teach Arabic if I found a couple of children. I thought of teaching Arabic at least to remember mother. But perhaps teaching is not for me.

My own children did not listen to me and they would evade me, making some excuse or the other. I don't have any other knowledge. I can't stitch chappals like Ramdas. Though I worked for four or five years in a shoe shop, I didn't even learn how to stitch chappals.

"No, anna. You have to get used to this job. You are people who read books. Big people," says Ramdas when I ask him to teach me the craft.

When I said this to Razia one day, she had looked me up and down. I can never forget those looks.

"Dheda ke saath dhedi aadatan…Moosa seth ke dukan me hisaban dekhlo. Roaming around with Madigas you have picked up Madiga[1] habits. Why don't you work in Moosa seth's shop and look after the accounts?" she had said harshly.

But hadn't I worked there for a while? Those account books wouldn't do now. Moosa seth would get angry for every small thing. He had removed me from work twice. With what face could I ask him for work again? "Ye hisab kitab ki tumhare zaroorat nai. These account books don't need you." Saying this, he had almost thrown the book at me. After he lost confidence in my memory, he had employed a youngster.

What else can I do?

There is not a place I did not go to. Not a place where I didn't enquire about work. When I would go for namaz, people would speak sympathetically and ask, but no one would ever give me employment even for a month!

I thought of teaching Arabic in the masjid. But the maulvi's son-in-law was already doing that.

"Anna, tell me what to do…everything is empty at home."

I say this each time I sit with Ramdas.

What can poor Ramdas say?

I love watching Ramdas stitching a chappal. When he stitches a chappal, he looks like a sculptor. When he sits holding the chappal and stitching it with utmost concentration, I wonder if I can do any work in life so steadily! Yes. When will my life become stable?

---

[1]**Madiga**: a Dalit community historically associated with leatherwork, tannery, making footwear and related crafts, and providing services such as the removal of animal carcasses, a majority work as agricultural labourers today. 'Madiga'—once an abusive, derogatory term associated with filth used for Dalits by non-Dalits—became a symbol of caste identity and self-respect after the Madiga Dandora movement in the 1990s. Madigas, together with Malas, comprise about 80 per cent of the Scheduled Caste population of Andhra Pradesh, and also have a sizable presence in Telangana and Karnataka.

Some lack of peace tortures me all the time. Mother fell seriously ill very unexpectedly. The only brother I had—quarrels in the village took his life. I reached this town like a madman. Except for this Ramdas, my small family and I have no other support. He was the only one I shared all my problems with. If I had to ask for anything, he was the only one.

I would not abstain even from a single namaz of the five I had to do. Those next to me who ensure that their shoulders are proper would not notice that my shoulders are slouching day by day with fear and poverty. Those who seek dua gidgidako, pleading in a trembling voice with tears in their eyes, would not be able to hear my sobs. As for that Parvardigare Aalam, He has never shown me the least sympathy. Whenever I say, "Arrehman nirraheem," tears fill my eyes and sobs rush to the throat. But His all merciful gaze has never turned towards me. Even so, as if I have bandaged my wounds, I do my namaz all five times of the day. The masjid feels like mother's lap. If I recite the namaz and complete a stanza, I feel that an invisible hand has for a moment gently patted me on my back and gone away.

As for me, the only God I can see is this "dhedee".

What does Razia know how much affection he holds beneath his dark skin? Except calling him "dhedee" in disgust! What does she know of him or the art in his hands?

Don't we have to pay at least hundred rupees if we want to buy new chappals? If a chappal falls into Ramdas's hands, no matter how old it is, it will turn into a new hundred-rupee chappal! After the asar namaz late afternoon, I come and sit next to Ramdas, immensely enjoy the tea he gets, and keep watching his hands working on those tattered old chappals. Razia says this is not art. She will come to know if I make her sit for an hour in front of Ramdas. Razia always felt like that towards Ramdas from the very beginning. We are from the same village. But even so, she will not raise her eyes and look at him. His body like a tumma[2] tree trunk,

[2]**tumma** or **nalla-tumma**: the babul tree, which has a rough brown bark and long sharp thorns.

his wild unruly greyish-black hair, his crooked legs, his manner of speaking—they all make her angry. One day when Ramdas brought food home, she threw it out right in front of him, saying, "Dhedee haath! Madiga hand!" But when he is stitching chappals, I feel like kissing his "dhedee haath". I feel like slicing off my own white, white hands.

Yes. What need of the wretched hands that cannot feed one's children even once? What should I do? Whether they stitch chappals, or they collect dung, or whatever they do, they are able to feed their children. What more does one need?

"What anna, where are you lost?" Ramdas says, cutting off my thoughts.

In the meanwhile, a youngster comes and stands before him in his black shoes.

Even as I watch, Ramdas polishes those shoes to make them shine like new. The youngster gives him five rupees and leaves.

With another ten rupees one can buy even white rice. My eyes are unable to see anything else now. Rice must be cooked at home. The children must eat to their stomachful and sleep. Razia must do her namaz without anger or irritation and remain calm.

Even as I am lost in my thoughts, a young girl comes and throws a pair of chappals in front of Ramdas, saying, "I'll come again. Please stitch these and keep them ready."

I look at Ramdas, wondering if he is upset at the way she threw them. But unconcerned, he is immediately immersed in his work.

No matter who comes or says anything, his work does not stop. This is a religious ritual for him.

"Anna, I will stitch this," I say with a lot of difficulty.

"Why, anna? If you need, I'll give you some money. Will I let your hands hold someone else's chappals?" he says, laughing.

True. Ramdas will not keep quiet if anyone says anything against me. In the village once during Sriramanavami, when someone slapped me, he went determined to that fellow's house and thrashed him. But in this town, everyone is hitting me hard on my stomach. Except feeling sorry, or helping us with a few grains sometimes, he too is unable to do anything more.

I pull the chappals from Ramdas's hands. I try hard, struggling for a while. What if the girl comes in the meanwhile…even so, it's okay. I stitch very courageously. Ramdas anna is instructing me. I am stitching. After stitching, when Ramdas has finished polishing, you have to see them then—the chappals are completely transformed! The girl comes. She wears the chappals. I fear she might throw them back at him. But she wears the slippers, pays him and leaves. Without even seeing how much it is, Ramdas puts the money in my hands.

"No, anna. I did it only because I had nothing to do."

"That's okay. If sister-in-law comes to know she will skin me alive and have slippers made out of my skin," says Ramdas.

As I am leaving, he puts another ten rupees in my pocket, even though I protest.

My eyes become wet.

I buy some rice and vegetables, and walk homewards.

Thanks to Ramdas, we will be able to tide over today.

But what if Razia asks where I got the money from? Even if it is just money, Razia will not touch it once she knows it has come from Ramdas.

As I am wondering what to say, I reach home.

There is some commotion inside. Both the children are making a lot of noise. Razia is unable to control them. There hasn't been such an atmosphere of play and merriment at home of late. Just as children would be excited when one makes chicken curry at home, that's the kind of excitement now.

As soon as I enter, Nasreen pulls me and makes me sit near her mother. In front of Razia there are four rotis and chicken curry.

"From where?" Even before I can ask her in surprise, Nasreen stuffs a bit of roti with chicken curry into my mouth, saying how wonderful it is!

Razia is sitting with her head bent.

I keep the packets of rice and vegetables in my hands next to the stove.

"From where...?" I ask.

What should I say? Should I tell him or not? I can't lie to him either..., she thinks.

Razia doesn't say a word.

The piece of roti and curry that Nasreen put into my mouth was indeed tasty.

"What to do? I have taken up housework."

A thunderbolt falls on my head. I somehow regain composure.

Now what should I say?

Razia takes a roti from the four kept in front of her and places it on another plate before me. In that roti, I see...Usman and his stringy beard...his dirty black body...his face sunken with penury. "Kya babujee...?" he asks me in his drawling voice.

"Aa?" I am startled.

Is he mocking me?

No.

The smile on his face is beautiful.

I am about to break the roti when both the children jump onto my back laughingly, wanting to play horse.

"Let abba eat!" Razia admonishes and pushes them away.

But I don't want their game to stop.

How many days has it been since I have seen the children laugh and clap like this! In fact right now I too feel like I am a child inside again. I somehow feel very peaceful...as if I am without any clothing, as if I have shed my pyjamas and kurta.

As if the body that went about by the old name of "Rafiq" that exuded a beautiful nawab-like attitude has been cast off, and that an ordinary man with a new name and a new head is flowing inside me. What shall I call this new person? Where are my education, my panchgana and my seerat, my inner beauty—I am unable to express all this in words. I am a father. I am a husband. I am an ordinary, a very ordinary man. I have no clothes on my body to tell me who I am. The black mark drawn on my forehead from doing namaz five times a day has been rubbed off. Has it really been rubbed off?

Perhaps not. But for now, I am far away from all that. I am like Usman—indifferent to everything.

"Arey badtameez! Khel-kood band karo! You insolent ones! Stop all this romping about!" Razia is shouting.

Is she saying this to me too? I suspect so.

She is holding our son Ajjugadu by the ear and pulling it angrily.

"Let him play! For how long will he play?" I say.

Are those my words? No. I have heard them somewhere before…from Usman.

But now those words do not reek of that foul odour. I can no longer smell that stench of attar on that old stained washed kurta when I recall them now.

"Usman…," I say aloud, as if I have woken up from a memory.

Both children look me up and down as if I am a madman.

Razia too.

"Sab ke sab…dhedeepan! Every one of you…afflicted by Madiga habits!" I can clearly hear Gorima scolding us from some corner.

Originally published in Telugu as 'Dhedee'
in *Prajatantra Vartamana Sahitya Sanchika*, 2002, pp. 132–142.

11. Chhoti Duniya

I get off from the University bus as usual.

On walking half a mile after getting down from the bus is our University Memorial Library. My routine is to study or write for a while in the library and then go for classes.

I like that half a mile walk immensely. Thinking about my educational goals, measuring my life path, I take each step slowly as I walk.

"Hey, Saher! Fast! Fast! You are worse than a snail!" Aarti always says.

There is a lot of difference between Aarti and me—aasmaan zameen farak, the difference between the sky and the earth. To walk with her is indeed to run! For me, for some reason, that run... it doesn't come from within me, it doesn't come from my feet. It doesn't come from my words either.

As to why I am studying this course? This question every day. The second question is why in fact am I in this country? True. No matter how much I invest in this course, the fact of the matter is that the result has not been good so far. It is a greater truth that no matter how long we remain in this country, our poverty will stick to us.

After this graduation, I must take off from further studies and work for a while. Have to see a bit of peace at home! That's the only dream I have as of now.

The minute I get down from the University bus today, the smell of the hijab I had tied around my face hits me strongly once again. I feel disgusted enough to want to pull off that stinking hijab and fling it out. My hands involuntarily try to pull it off my head a couple of times and put it into the bag, but some thoughts restrain those hands…I am unable to take it off that easily. A suspicion that the entire world is looking piercingly at me time and again. But I know that those who are going that way don't have even a minute's leisure to lift up their eyes and look. Even so, I feel as if all eyes have fallen on me!

"Don't have coins to put in the laundry, Chhoti! Now there is no time even to wash and put it to dry. Put up with it somehow today!" Saying this, ammee wrapped the faded hijab around my head and continued, "The times are really not good. A country not our country…a language not ours…a country where we don't have our people…we must always be on our guard." I felt like saying, "But there is no connection between hijab and security!"

"When you go out, don't ever forget to read the Ayatul Kursi, Chhoti! If you read that dua and blow it onto the body, no shaitan wind will blow your way!" Ammee would remind me every time I stepped out. "Ammee, this is America!" I had told her many times, and coming to the conclusion that there was no faida in saying it, I would keep quiet.

Ammee's firm belief is that America is fully a shaitan country. So, why are we here? This is what my elder maternal uncle did as soon as he became a citizen—drag us to America! Though my mother kept objecting, Rafi mamu did not pay heed, and at first thought that we would tide over the difficulties if we worked in a restaurant for some time. But it is not clear even to this day whether those difficulties have been overcome or we are beset with new difficulties.

In these seven years, America has changed a lot. But ammee… wasn't ammee the same even when we were in Hyderabad? In her eyes, the whole place is full of shaitans! She looks very suspiciously, no matter at whom! She won't mingle with anyone till she has given it a lot of thought! Why ammee became like that I will tell you in another story.

When I took Aarti home for the first time, ammee immediately took me into the kitchen and said, "Are there no Muslim girls in your college for you to make dosts with?" It never struck me until then that Aarti was Hindu. Did it really not strike me? Or perhaps the thought must have flown away somewhere during our friendship.

Though I am saying this about ammee, and though I tell myself many times, "This is America," I am in fact no better than her! When I don't have the hijab on my head, I feel suffocated! Will I be able to at least walk up to the grocery store on this very street in the next lane without my hijab? That is how accustomed I have got to it! As to how accustomed, why, I am tolerating that dirty hijab even today.

Normally, I love to walk these twenty-five steps. Perhaps I did not sleep well last night. I keep yawning as I walk. This dirty hijab...the frequent yawns because of feeling sleepy...Each step feels so heavy!

Meanwhile...loud shouts from the Capitol area at a short distance. Big crowds. Hmm, so again this problem! Around the Capitol, huge crowds, protest tents, shouts of "Occupy...!" I believe it is a movement. Though I haven't yet figured out what kind of a movement it is. Total commotion on TV and radio. It seems it is a war against economic inequality. Will that ever be resolved? Is it necessary to make such a hue and cry for the impossible? Today my tuitions have been completely washed out. Is this a government that doesn't even allow teaching to continue?! A government making education into a big capital, a big business, and taking it to such extremes...! Republicans, Democrats...has anyone ever paid heed to this? Please just allow me to study a little. That is enough for me.

"You and studies are poles apart! Are you even capable of doing safai work in Pakistani restaurants?" abbajaan had said impatiently. For everything, "Pakistani"! Constantly being stamped a Pakistani, I might even forget that I am an Indian! The other day a girl called out to me mockingly, "Hey you Paki!" Muslim means Paki—that's what everyone here understands. How grossly unfair!

"How do you know I am a Paki?" I'd felt like giving her one on her face! "No...Never do that. These are not good times for Muslims. Patience—the only weapon Allah has given us," ammee had said in some context.

As I approach the Occupied Camp, the stench kills the nostrils. In the vicinity of the camp, there's a peculiar odour...a terrible stink...as if a hijab hadn't been washed for months! Felt peculiar.

Ya Allah! I think to myself and walk past swiftly.

"Sometimes, also stop for a while and see what is happening there, Saher...Meri pyari chhoti duniya, my sweet little world," Aarti says. When she is very angry with me or when she is very affectionate, she teases me sometimes by calling me "chhoti duniya," like they do at home.

"No—all that is just a duniya of lazy people!" I say, and keep quiet. Aarti remains silent. Then, as we near the library, I sense that she wants to say something. But there is no time to talk now. If I don't submit the paper by this evening, Professor Syed will deduct points.

"Saher, this is all a game. You've got to learn this! Just play, play and play! No one here sees where you come from. They only consider whether at this moment you are playing as well as them or not. If the ball slips, the game is over!" Professor Syed had once laughingly told me.

I have great regard for Professor Syed. Rather than exams that resemble quiz questions, a teacher who teaches students to sharpen their thinking, making them write papers and reading each and every word carefully, writing down his comments in detail...such professors who love their students are very rare.

"But how do you play this game? The grammar of this game is entirely your choice. You have to choose, Saher. You have to figure it out. No one will tell you how. The system only wants results. That's all. Not your failure!"

True. But when my failure becomes the chains that bind my feet every moment, when it dictates my present even without my initiative...then, what should I do?

"Professor, in fact, even now this doesn't appear to be my world. I who had studied in some remote corner in the old city, as life chased me crazily, I came and fell like a ball here. I am someone who hadn't heard a complete sentence in English till my ninth class. Yes. I did not know any world other than Urdu. I even speak to the computer in Urdu. I have never been a brilliant student. Very average. And I don't know why, but I do not have that competitive spirit in me. From the very beginning. And by the way, where does that spirit even come from? I have never understood that. If I eat one time, unable to eat another time, if I buy one class textbook, unable to buy another, if I pay school fees one month, unable to pay the next month...then, who should I compete with?"

When I had joined this course, and submitted a written essay the very first week, I wanted to burst out crying in front of Professor Syed after what he said. "Saher, you are writing Urdu in English! It is difficult to write in the second language. Yes, I know. But you must learn how to write! You must write a little every day! If you like, go to the Writing Center and get all your work edited," he said these words straight to my face. But the truth is that this whole world is like a second language to me.

What he said after that wrenched my heart. "Your problem is not just the language, but thought, too! Language is different, thought is different. If your thought is clear, your language will be clear. You are not thinking clearly, Saher," he spelt it out, looking keenly into my eyes.

Afterwards I do not recall how much time or how many hours I spent talking to Aarti in that state of mind. Finally she said, "Don't be so emotional, Saher, try and look at it more objectively. Just think a little about what he said, and we'll talk again tomorrow."

On such a night, abbajaan threw another boulder at my heart. "Take this semester off. You can resume after I get a job. I am not able to cope with all this expenditure."

It is no surprise that abbajaan should speak like this. He does not have even the small job that he had in the grocery store till the other day. When he lost the job two months ago, he did not have even the money to pay a month's rent. So mother had to finally take up a part-time job in a Pakistani restaurant. The money she gets is not enough to buy groceries for the house. By the time it comes to tuition fees, it appears as if she must pawn her head.

"Dear Professor, you said it was enough if I posted two questions for tomorrow's class. But tonight I have at least ten questions before me—I wonder if you or the President of America could answer them...Nevertheless, I am happy that in this country there is at least the freedom to ask questions!"

Having sent this in an email to the professor at midnight, I fall back lifeless on the sofa! Have to see what he has to say. Those words...I want just those few words. Words that will enliven these weak moments. It doesn't matter from whom they come...It doesn't matter if it is from any dark corner of the world that surrounds me!

Slumping onto the sofa, I try to open a book.

But those questions are juggling indifferently with my thoughts. Questions have no sympathy for anyone. For that matter, no one sympathises with another here. Work...work... work...If the work done is good, praise. No one forgives your failures. But they will pass judgments on your failures and on your personality.

Yes. There can be no respite for the many balls that must be juggled! Must keep all the balls up in the air...ten balls, only two hands! Must speak with Aarti tomorrow! "Not just me—you must also speak ruthlessly with yourself!" Aarti had said as her parting words last night.

Speaking with myself means...Is this a solvable problem?

I get up early, get ready quickly and set out for the campus. I called Aarti earlier, to say that we will sit at the Union Café after classes.

After classes get over at three, as I am about to sit down at the Union Café, Aarti comes, wearing a nice light red T-shirt. Her T-shirts are always good. In fact I too want to wear a T-shirt like her and go about—not with a dress inside and again on top of it this burkha! Once in a while I do get irritated.

The words on Aarti's T-shirt are also good. Wondering what's on her T-shirt today, I lean forward and read. *If hope is an impossible demand, then we demand the impossible*—these words are printed in yellow.

"Hmm...that's nice...a very good line!" I say.

"Do you like it...really? Those are Judith Butler's words. Not mine!" says Aarti. "Okay, will you have coffee or tea? *It's my treat!*"

She knows I don't have the courage to spend three dollars on coffee. "No," I say, embarrassed.

"Don't be embarrassed, thallee! We don't have coffee here every day, do we? It's Starbucks coffee...just try it! You stay here and take care of the seats. I'll go get them quickly." Saying this, Aarti goes to the Starbucks counter, brings two cups of coffee, and sits down saying, "Bolo...tell me."

Where shall I start? I am being sucked into silence. Aarti knows my condition. No matter what, she is a Senior. She will complete her studies this year. Moreover, she thinks very clearly, and from all angles, before I can even gather my thoughts.

"How are things at home?" she asks.

"Not good. Ammee is irritated. To go out like that and work—ammee doesn't like it at all. Abbajaan is working an hour here, an hour there. That's not stable either. I don't know what will happen to my studies. The tuition fee is increasing."

"Chhoti, all these things will be resolved somehow or the other. Even if you worry about them, there's nothing you can do. But what you have to worry about is yourself."

I look questioningly into Aarti's eyes.

"Yes. This education is a great opportunity for you. Education does not mean only getting good grades and graduating quickly. Though that is important, no doubt."

"That's what is most important to me. But my grades are coming down. Why coming down, when were they good anyway!"

"You must get good grades, true. I don't disagree. But not just in your studies. You are now also at that corner from where your personality will take a turn. You are also a bit confused at this point!"

"Means...?"

"Means, read the words on this T-shirt once again."

"Umm...*If hope is an impossible demand, then we demand the impossible*. That's good!"

"But there is a continuation to it. *If hope is an impossible demand, then we demand the impossible. If the right to shelter, food and employment are impossible demands, then we demand the impossible.*"

"Are these your words?"

"Do you have so much faith in my brains? These are Judith Butler's words. Tonight, go back and google and find out who she is. I'll email you the speech that she gave at the meeting in New York. Read it. Think about it."

"Why do I need to know all that?"

"That is precisely what your problem is—this kind of attitude. Not just yours, it is the problem of many of our people here. We think that the world is very big. But in fact it is a very small world. Ekdam chhoti duniya! If you just think about it a bit, from our hometown to New York, it is the same world, the same problems, the same turmoil. Here Occupy, there Telangana! That's all! It just won't do to say that we will be like cats on the wall. These are the challenges. These are the questions that ask you to find out who you are. Now everyone's situation is the same. Everyone's anxiety is the same. But each one of us has his or her own identity. You are not realising that. If we don't realise that, then there is no meaning to our education. ...Ammo, this lecture has gone on too long! But this is essentially what I wanted to say."

"I don't know...! But I am unable to see the point in any of those things. Even if I do see them, I feel that those problems are not related to me."

"You cannot escape, Saher. That is not your choice. This is a time when migration is inevitable. Your abbajaan lived in some village near Khammam. Why did he go to Hyderabad? Once migration begins, it is no longer in your hands. Till there is land beneath our feet, we will keep moving. But whether or not we are ready for the lessons that the new land teaches us is what is important."

I keep nodding my head. "You spoke of identity earlier. Do we really have an identity in a country not our own...in a language not our own...?"

"Why not? Identity is greater than a country or a language. But teenagers like us who come to the university campus—of course I am not a teenager now—more importantly those teenagers who have migrated don't know how to search for their identity. If many of us are Hindus, we join the Hindu Students' Council. If they are Muslims, they gather around the campus masjid. Without our knowledge we get drawn into those labels, and we create a little India or a little Pakistan. That same Gita, that same Quran, that same pooja, that same namaz then become our identity markers. Our search for identity ends right there. For if we go beyond that, we don't feel comfortable, because it is not our comfort zone."

"What's wrong with that?"

"There's nothing wrong with that. But it is wrong to think that that alone is completely right. Have you ever thought what you are after those meetings? No. No one thinks. Are you really a Hindu? Really a Muslim? As for me, I think it is only a half truth. In fact, the remaining half is dependent on how well you become one with the soil around you. Have you seen the people who are sitting near the Capitol shouting slogans? Don't you see the earnestness in those screams?"

"No. They are all homeless! Hopeless people! They are lazy and unwilling to work hard. So they are doing sit-ins and squatting there!" I say emphatically.

"Have you spoken to any of them?"

"No."

"Then how can you say so?"

"I have heard ammee, abba and our friends talking about it. Some of our dosts who come home have also said so."

"Not they, you. What do *you* think?"

"I don't think about it. I have no time for it or the patience!"

"Don't get offended by my words, Saher—but this is a typical desi mindset! Do you remember how bad you felt the other day at Professor Syed's words?"

"Yes."

"That's not just about you. Not just about your writing. It is about all of us who are terrified at the idea of thinking..."

"I am not afraid of thinking. But where do I have the time to think? All the time is taken up with studies. Competition... competition. Somehow I must get into medical college."

"No, you can't think only of studies. Only of grades. Only of marks. Only of career. You have to also think about experiences. Also think about incidents. Why are our professors shouting hoarse that we must have critical thinking? If you don't have critical thinking your understanding will not improve. You won't be able to understand yourself. You won't even be able to move an inch from your comfort zone!"

"Why should I move out?"

"If you don't move out, you won't progress! You think that the tuition fee is just your problem? Your abbajaan losing a monthly salary, being left with just daily wages, and sometimes not even that, your ammee going out to work even though she doesn't want to... all these are not just your problems, Saher. Thinking that they are makes them look like demons to you. They isolate you and frighten you!"

"Ammo! This sounds too complicated to me!"

"No. That's why you have to speak to yourself. You have to introspect for a while. That's the great training these studies give us! Reflexivity—if we learn just that, the rest will follow."

Coffee is over. The discussion has not come to any conclusion. Perhaps it may not. But Aarti can speak like this for any length of time. Then why can't I? Why don't these ideas occur to me? I must at least be able to think clearly in this manner. Have to be able to speak. Have to speak out loud.

Aarti's words are causing a turmoil within me. It's not so easy to tap and wake up my dull brain! But Aarti knows the art of speaking! Even if you keep tapping and hit hard, not a sentence comes out of me. But Aarti knows how to tap thoughts.

Perhaps another sleepless night awaits me!

Why can't I come out of my comfort zone? Is it because of my inner fears? Is it because I am unable to tolerate the possibility of a commotion outside of this restricted space? Does everything I do reside in this comfort zone?

The night bird chirps peacefully at two on the clock, as if to say, now go to bed.

I don't even know what I am thinking. So many thoughts and anxieties are overpowering me like boulders—but, this thought does not irritate me. It does not make me agitated. Each layer of thoughts parades silently in front of my mind as if each layer is being peeled off one by one. Yes, these moments are heavy, but the mind feels light and steady.

This may not be a big battle. But there is a feeling of satisfaction as if I have won a battle.

I write just one sentence in my journal and slide into sleep.

"Put it in perspective."

When I get up in the morning, brush my teeth and look at my face in the mirror, it appears fresh, clean and pure to me.

Originally published in Telugu as 'Chhoti Duniya'
in *Aadivaram Andhra Jyothy*, 7 October 2012, pp. 143–154.